"He's a be... whispered.

Rachel didn't answer. She didn't want to break the spell.

As they stood side by side gazing down at the sleeping baby, she suddenly felt an amazing closeness.

This is what it would be like if Charlie had a father, she thought. *It would be good to share this beautiful boy with someone who loved him as much as I do. With someone who loved me, too.*

Jack slowly turned toward her and looked into her eyes, as if he could read her mind. His hands rose and gently touched her hair.

If there was a time to step back, this was it.

But she couldn't move a muscle.

Dear Reader,

What is it about babies?

What is the mysterious quality that can melt even the most distant, reserved personality into a warm, sticky puddle of cooing affection?

My own "baby" is now a preteen, with all the trimmings—messy room, iPod, piles of homework and assorted sports equipment.

When I first had the idea for this trilogy, BABY DAZE, it was hard to remember those early years. Then a friend had a child and it all came back in a rush. The smell of that little head just after a bath, the gurgling laugh, the sensation of being fed Cheerios by tiny fingers.

Maybe part of the mystery is simply how babies so easily inspire loving feelings. No wonder they appear so often in romance novels.

I hope you enjoy *Dad in Disguise,* the story of a woman who yearns for a baby and makes great sacrifices to be a mother. And a man who never realized how much he wants a child…until he finds out he's a father.

Happy reading,

Kate Little

DAD IN DISGUISE

KATE LITTLE

SPECIAL EDITION®

Published by Silhouette Books

America's Publisher of Contemporary Romance

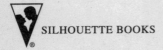

SILHOUETTE BOOKS

ISBN-13: 978-0-373-24889-6
ISBN-10:   0-373-24889-X

DAD IN DISGUISE

Copyright © 2008 by Anne Canadeo

This edition published by arrangement with Harlequin Books S.A.

® and TM are trademarks of Harlequin Books S.A., used under license.
Trademarks indicated with ® are registered in the United States Patent
and Trademark Office, the Canadian Trade Marks Office and in other
countries.

Visit Silhouette Books at www.eHarlequin.com

Printed in U.S.A.

KATE LITTLE

claims to have lots of experience with romance—
"the *fictional* kind, that is," she is quick to clarify.
She has been both an author and an editor of
romance fiction for over fifteen years. She believes
that a good romance will make the reader experience
all the tension, thrills and agony of falling madly,
deeply and wildly in love. Kate enjoys watching the
characters in her books go crazy for each other, but
she hates to see the blissful couple disappear when
it's time for them to live happily ever after.

In addition to writing romance novels, Kate also
writes fiction and nonfiction for young adults. She
lives on Long Island with her husband and daughter.

Chapter One

You never know what's going to happen when you wake up in the morning.

You think you do…but you don't.

That's what Jack Sawyer believed now. Less than a week ago, he'd opened an innocent-looking envelope and his life changed in the blink of an eye.

Settled at his desk on a typical Monday morning, he was sorting through a pile of mail while sipping his coffee and a letter marked "Personal & Confidential" caught his eye.

He tore it open, read it and—bam!

A meteor might have landed smack dab in the middle of his sleekly decorated executive office. In the middle of his sleekly decorated life.

The letter had come from a firm called Dynamics, Inc. He couldn't place it at first. When he finally did, he cringed.

Dynamics, Inc. was a sperm bank where he'd impulsively made a donation two years ago. It had been a bleak, frightening moment in his life. Diagnosed with an inoperable tumor, the prognosis had been grim. Given only a few months to live, Jack faced a sad truth. For all his accomplishments and worldly success, he wondered if he'd achieved very much at all. For one thing, he'd never married and had children, a fact he deeply regretted at that moment.

There had been plenty of lovely, marriageable women in his life and plenty of chances for commitment. Maybe too many choices. Jack didn't know why, but something always held him back. Somehow, at the last minute, he always sidestepped walking down the aisle, claiming he wasn't ready. Or deciding that the woman in question just wasn't "The One." Maybe he just didn't want to make the changes a real commitment would demand.

His lifestyle wasn't suited to marriage…and maybe his temperament wasn't either, he thought. He'd bounced around foster homes most of his childhood, some kind and some cruel.

He'd never felt part of a real family and had never known close, loving ties. No wonder he thought relationships were hard. Work was easy and life was never boring, traveling to the world's greatest cities, where his skills and vision as an architect were always in demand.

But during that dark time, Jack couldn't kid himself. No one really cared who designed a skyscraper or even a monument. Children were the real legacy. Without that bequest to the future, all his worldly accomplishments didn't amount to much.

Or so Jack had felt as he faced his mortality. Donating to a sperm bank seemed some small consolation. There had been some extra scrutiny, due to his medical situation, but finally, he was accepted as a donor. Jack had been thankful and relieved. If he was going to leave this world without having children the traditional way, at least his DNA—and perhaps even some portion of his spirit—would live on.

A few weeks later, Jack happily learned he wasn't a doomed man after all. A cloud on his MRI had caused his condition to be misdiagnosed and his tests results had been inaccurate. With luck, he would live a long life and had time enough to marry and have children if he wanted...the usual way.

Jack sat back and had a good laugh. A sperm bank? What in the world had he been thinking?

He contacted Dynamics, Inc. immediately and withdrew his donation. The organization told him that his genetic material was never given out and Jack was relieved to hear it.

And that was that.

Or so he thought.

Now, two years later, the laboratory had written that they'd made a mistake. A recent audit revealed that Jack's sperm had in fact been administered at least once before it was removed from the bank.

It took Jack a few moments to consider the full implications. Once he did, he was nearly blown out of his cushy leather desk chair.

Some unknown woman out there could have become pregnant with his "donation" and given birth to his baby!

What did this all mean? What should he do? Could he even find out this woman's identity and what had happened to her?

Within seconds, Jack was on the phone to his attorneys. "Why look for trouble?" he was told. "The chances are incredibly slim, Jack. Less than one in a million."

Jack had to agree. But he couldn't let it rest. He felt nagged by a strange stirring, down deep in his gut. He had to know for sure if this particular long shot had come in. The information was confidential, but the high-powered law firm that represented him was good at pulling strings and coaxing open sealed files.

After a few days of anxious waiting, his gut instinct was

validated. Jack was stunned to learn that he was indeed a father.

Rachel Reilly was the child's mother and the baby, a little boy born about ten months ago, she'd named Charlie. But the investigators hired by Jack's attorneys had found out precious little more.

Rachel Reilly was single, twenty-nine years old, a clothing designer who specialized in children's wear. She'd been living in Manhattan and working for the same clothing company since she'd graduated college. But a few months ago, she sold her city apartment, pooled all her savings—including a small inheritance from her mother's recent death—and bought a house in Vermont. The small village she'd chosen was just over the New York state border. She'd quit her job and moved there.

Jack couldn't believe it. All these months, at least until recently, he'd been living in the same city as this Mystery Mom and his own son. He could have passed them on the street, sidestepping the baby's stroller. Now that he'd known they existed, they were in the middle of nowhere. Where in the world was Blue Lake? He'd dug out a road atlas and could barely find it, a tiny dot in the midst of the Berkshires.

Barely twenty-four hours after receiving the investigator's report, Jack was on his way, and the same map sat crumpled on the passenger's seat beside him. Against all the good advice he'd been given, Jack refused to send a professional investigator. He knew had to follow this trail himself, wherever it might lead. He had to see his son and this mystery mother firsthand, not the blurry image taken through a tele-photo lense.

He'd been driving for hours and had turned off the highway some time ago, traveling now on narrow two-lane roads that wound through the mountains and valleys of southern Vermont. It was late September and cooler than it had been down in New York City, the hillsides looking as if they'd been lightly touched with a paint brush.

He drove through wooded stretches and small towns and through valleys where the view opened up to green pastures dotted with big red barns and lazy-looking cows. Lush green trees arched over head and handmade signs on the roadside advertised Pick your own apples and Fresh Eggs, Milk & Cheese, reminding Jack he hadn't eaten anything since he'd left the city early that morning. But he didn't want to stop, too intent on reaching his destination.

He knew he had to be close to Blue Lake by now. Close to seeing his son.

Charlie. He liked the name. He said it out loud to himself in the car, over and over again.

Jack couldn't wait to see the little guy with his own eyes. To touch him, or hold him. To hear the sounds he made, even the crying. He didn't have any trouble picturing the boy. It was simple. Jack envisioned a miniature version of himself. Logically he knew it may not have turned out that way, but he couldn't help it.

He did have trouble picturing Rachel Reilly. What did she look like? Was she tall or short? Dark or fair? Slim or curvy?

More importantly, what kind of woman was she? What kind of woman opts to get pregnant through a sperm bank, anyway? Some homely, lonely, forever single type, without any hope of having kids the usual way? Some radical Amazon who holds a grudge against men on principle? Some uptight prude who just hates sex, period?

He didn't want his son to be raised by any of the above. He wasn't sure what his rights were in the situation, but he had money. Plenty of money. For better or worse, it's not the best man who wins, Jack had learned, but usually the guy who can afford the best lawyers.

Even if she wasn't some nut case or recluse, what kind of mother was she? Jack had barely known his own mother before being dumped into the social service system. He couldn't stand the idea of his boy being raised by any woman who was less than ideal—who wasn't warm, nurturing, loving. All the things a mother should be.

If Rachel Reilly wasn't a good mother—wasn't a *great* mother—he'd get his son away from her before you could say *X chromosome*.

No matter what it took.

Finally, a sign for Blue Lake appeared on the roadside. Jack turned and found himself driving down the town's Main Street. He cruised down the avenue slowly, surprised to see the quaint, old-fashioned architecture—well-kept shops and restaurants on a busy main thoroughfare. There were awnings and flower boxes, wrought-iron street lamps and a town square with a big white gazebo in the middle.

If Rachel Reilly had to stick herself in the middle of nowhere, at least she picked a pleasant middle of nowhere. He scanned the numbers on the doorways, trying to find her address. Finally at the end of the thoroughfare, he came to number 533, a Queen Anne style Victorian with a wraparound porch and a turret on the third floor.

Freshly painted, the house was an eye-popping combination of pale pink with magenta shutters and a yellow door with touches of violet blue and bright white trim. Just this side of overdone, but the English style garden in front and white picket fence lent an overall effect that was fanciful and stunning.

A hand painted wooden sign hung from a post in the middle of the garden:

Pretty Baby—Unique treasures for babies & toddlers ~ Clothing, Toys, Furniture and More! ~ Made with a loving touch.

A loving touch. He liked that phrase. So far, so good.

But Rachel Reilly might not have anything to do with this store. He couldn't jump to conclusions.

There was plenty of space to park in front, but Jack drove down the street and chose a spot out of sight. His car—which cost more than most people made in a year—seemed as conspicuous as a rocket ship. He didn't want to draw attention to himself if he could help it.

The information from the investigators hadn't included anything about a baby store. He studied the house some more, deciding there must be an apartment on the second and third floor. Maybe she lived up there. Maybe he should just sit and wait for her to come in or out of the building, like a real PI would do.

But Jack had never been big on patience. He'd driven all day and was dying to catch even a glimpse of his son. Maybe someone working in there could give him some information.

He checked his image in the rearview mirror. Chocolate brown eyes stared back at him. He never had trouble attracting women and more than a few had told him he was handsome. But Jack didn't see it. Especially not today.

He'd started the drive early and now looked worn out and even needed a shave. Well, there was no help for it. The grubby look was sort of country-like, wasn't it? Helped him blend in with the scenery?

Pocketing his car keys, he and climbed out. At the last minute, he pulled off his leather jacket, trading it for a gray sweatshirt he spotted behind the driver's seat. He tugged it on and pulled up the zipper. There, instant "working man," he thought. His black T-shirt was expensive but nondescript. His jeans had cost a small fortune, but had the fashionable worn out look that wouldn't give him away.

He didn't like the feeling of going "undercover" like this. Deception wasn't part of his character. But under the circumstances, it was probably wiser. He didn't know anything about this woman beyond the bare essentials. He had to find out more about her before he could decide what to do.

She held all the cards in her hand.

She had his son.

* * *

The sound of the bell on the shop door made Charlie stir in her arms. He'd just about dropped off but the noise disturbed him. Now she'd have to pace a few more moments—while singing a few more verses of "Rockin' Robin"—before he would conk out and she could set him down in his portacrib.

This mother-shopskeeper juggling act was tricky. Some days it seemed like a complete disaster. But she had made the right choice, Rachel kept reminding herself. Things would work out. Eventually.

Having Charlie with her in the store hadn't seemed to hurt sales any. Most people enjoyed seeing a real live baby amidst the baby paradise she'd created in Pretty Baby.

If some customers got impatient or even walked out, what could she do? Charlie was her priority. She'd purposely designed the shop—designed her entire life—so that her son came first. He was with her all day and had his own daycare room where he could sleep, eat, play and do everything a ten-month-old needed to do.

Besides, it was best to let them browse a while before she pounced. There was so much to look at, most people forgot what they'd come in for.

Rachel hummed and paced and soon felt Charlie's body heavy and slack, his breathing deep. She set him down gently and tiptoed to the doorway.

"I'll be right with you. Just one more second," she called out softly to her customer.

"No problem" a deep male voice called back.

Rachel returned to Charlie and pulled a light blanket over him. Men shopping alone at her store were unusual. They rarely had any idea of what they wanted, or even the age and size of the baby they were buying for, looking a little lost among the tiny outfits and fluffy toys. They would put themselves totally at her mercy and take just about anything she suggested.

It was tempting, but she never took advantage of them.

Sure that Charlie was finally asleep, Rachel lightly kissed his forehead, inhaling his sweet baby scent, then stepped out into the shop. She spotted her customer wandering around the toy section. He didn't look the type who would whip out a gold Am Ex card and put her in the black for the month. But there hadn't been much business today and she welcomed the sight of him. And what a sight indeed.

He was tall, with thick dark hair and impossibly broad shoulders, outlined by a gray sweatshirt jacket he wore over a T-shirt and worn jeans. The floppy velour bunny in his hand—one of her handmade originals—seemed totally out of synch with his dark intensity. He looked over at her, his brown eyes curious, taking her in, his expression unreadable.

Rachel felt self-conscious and pushed her curly hair back from her face with her hand. Between the store and Charlie, she didn't have much time to bother about her appearance. The past few months, she'd gone from urban chic to basic hygiene. But what could you do? Out here in Blue Lake, she didn't worry about things like that. Not the way she did while living in the city.

Rachel quickly checked her T-shirt and denim long skirt, looking for apple sauce or spit up stains. All clear. That was some comfort. Summoning her best shopkeeper smile, she stepped forward. "Hi. Can I help you with something?"

He didn't answer right away. He looked at the stuffed rabbit in his hand and quickly put it down.

"I'm just browsing. I was passing through town and thought I'd stop in and take a look around. The store is very…eye-catching."

"Thanks." Rachel smiled, not sure he meant it as a compliment. "I thought the painted lady look might be too much. But it does attract attention."

He nodded. "Just about stops traffic. Is this your shop?"

Rachel smiled proudly. "I opened about a month ago."

"Very nice. You make all this stuff yourself?"

"I design most of the clothes and toys. I look for other items that are handmade or really unique. And I paint all the furniture. I do room murals, too," she said, glancing over at the far wall that was painted with a scene of a nursery rhyme, "Hey Diddle, Diddle." The opposite side of the store was painted with the tea party scene from *Alice In Wonderland* and behind the cash register, there was a magical, misty garden, filled with flowers and fairies.

"You're very talented."

Rachel smiled and shrugged. "I'm okay. Painting is the fun part. I haven't gotten any calls yet for the wall murals, but business is picking up."

He didn't say anything, just slowly smiled, deep dimples creasing his lean cheeks that were touched with five o'clock shadow. He had a dimple in his chin, too, she noticed. Just like Charlie. She wondered if her son would grow up to be half as handsome as this guy. She'd have to teach him not to be a heartbreaker.

"Do you own the building, or just lease this space?"

The question seemed a little odd, but maybe the guy was into real estate or thinking of opening a shop in town himself. "I own the building," she said simply.

Before she could say more, Charlie's sharp cry cut through the air. The man turned to listen, his expression shocked, as if he'd never heard a baby before.

"That's my son. He's taking a nap. Or *was* taking a nap. Can you excuse me, please? I'll be right back."

"That's okay… You'd better go check on him." The man watched her dash off. Still looking stunned. Surprised she had her baby with her? Maybe…

Rachel ran back to the nursery and scooped Charlie up in her arms, patting his back to comfort him. She checked his diaper and found it dry. His pacifier subdued the sobs, but there seemed no sense trying to settle him down again. The little stinker was wide awake. And she had a customer waiting. She grabbed his comfort toy, a white dog with a spot over one eye, and dashed out to the shop again.

Her customer stood near the counter, right where she'd left him. He had his back to her, but quickly turned when he heard her steps.

"This is Charlie. He likes to be where the action is," Rachel said, introducing them.

"Hello, Charlie. Hey, guy…I'm your…I'm Jack. "

He spoke quietly, staring at Charlie in the oddest way. Then looked up at her and blinked, his eyes suddenly glassy. The color drained from his lean cheeks and he suddenly looked pale as paper. Rachel feared he was about to faint.

She reached out and touched his arm. "Are you all right? Do you want to sit down?"

He forced a smile and shook his head. Then took a deep breath and straightened to his full height again.

"I'm okay. Honest. I've been driving all day. Must have drunk too much coffee."

"Maybe," Rachel agreed, still feeling concerned. "Would you like some water?"

"No, thanks. I'm fine now. See?" He smiled at her again, looking embarrassed at his momentary lapse.

Wow, he was handsome. It had been a boring day, but this guy sure made up for it.

He was looked down at Charlie again, then met her gaze. He swallowed hard before he spoke. "Your little boy is beautiful. How old is he?"

"Ten months. I made a nursery for him down here in the shop so he can hang out with me all day."

"That's nice… So, you don't believe in daycare?"

Rachel shrugged. "I used to work in an office and Charlie was with a nanny. Nine to five, and even longer. I hardly saw him. After a few months, I knew I had to figure out something different. Something that was right for me. I'm all he's got," she added.

She wasn't sure why she'd told him that last part. What did it matter to him if she was single, or not? She usually preferred not to even go there. People had too many prying questions.

He didn't though, luckily.

He didn't say anything in reply, but was still staring at her, studying her with that odd, amazed look on his face. It made her feel self-conscious. Maybe she reminded him of somebody?

"By the way, my name is Rachel Reilly." Rachel set Charlie down in a seat on the counter top between them. Jack watched as she strapped the baby in.

"Jack Sawyer," he said. "I'm pleased to meet you, Rachel."

His expression seemed serious again. His dark gaze met hers and held it. Rachel felt something flash between them. Some flash of attraction that went deep, the kind she hadn't felt in a long time.

The phone rang, calling her back to reality. Rachel looked over at it, but didn't pick it up. Jack Sawyer had been her only customer this afternoon, but so far, she'd spent little time trying to sell him anything.

"You can pick it up if you like. I'm not in a rush."

Rachel hesitated a second, then reached for the phone. Jack turned his full attention to Charlie, who had grasped his stuffed dog in two hands and now kicked his feet so hard one of his blue and white striped socks was slipping off.

Rachel picked up the phone, answering it with a smile. "Pretty Baby. May I help you?"

"Miss Reilly? It's George Nolan. Sorry it took so long to get back to you."

Rachel's good mood instantly curdled. "Mr. Nolan, thanks for finally returning my calls," *My many, many calls.* "So, what's going on? Are you going to do the roof or not?"

Rachel could tell from the long silent pause on the other end of the line that the answer was not going to be the one she hoped for. She'd hired George Nolan to put a new roof on the cottage at the back of her property and fix the water damage inside. He'd been due to start the job last week. He'd put her off with a hundred excuses and finally, just stopped answering her phone calls.

"I'm sorry, Miss Reilly. I have to be straight with you," he began. It's about time, Rachel thought.

"A big renovation job ahead of yours got backed up and I'm down two men on my crew. I'm not going to get over to your place before, say…three, maybe four weeks."

"Three or four weeks? That's impossible. You said the work would done by then."

"Sorry about that, but it can't be helped. Excuse me a minute. I'll be right back."

Rachel gave out a long frustrated sigh. It was annoying enough to be totally dissed by her contractor. Then to be put on hold while he weaseled out of the job seemed too much to bear.

But he was a man, what could you expect? Even the seemingly nice ones couldn't be trusted. That's the lesson she'd learned.

Charlie would be different. She'd make sure of it. He'd be the one man in a million a woman could trust and depend on. She gave him a loving glance as he squealed and tossed his dog. Rachel moved to pick it up, but Jack was faster. He quickly retrieved the stuffed animal, carefully brushed if off with his large hand and gently offered it to the baby again.

Charlie grabbed it and Jack sat back with a big silly grin.

"Great reflexes. You're going to be some athlete. A pitcher or maybe a full back?" Jack's deep soft tone was both admiring and serious.

Charlie stared at Jack, then tossed the dog again, this time even harder. Jack tilted his head back and laughed. He picked up the toy once more and gave it back to Charlie.

"He'll make you do that all day if you don't watch out," Rachel warned.

Jack looked up at her, smiling. "I don't mind. He's got a great arm. You'll have to get him into Little League right away."

Rachel laughed. "Absolutely. I think he has to learn walk first though. I don't think he can try out if he has to crawl around the bases."

Jack Sawyer smiled briefly but didn't reply. Rachel hadn't meant to be sarcastic, but it was typical of a guy to make that sort of comment. Men were so competitive. Always trying to force boys into sports. She wouldn't be like that with Charlie. He'd only play sports if he wanted to. It didn't matter to her one way or the other.

"Miss Reilly? You still there?" George Nolan came back on the line.

"I'm still here, Mr. Nolan."

"I'm sorry about this delay. But it can't be helped. If you can find another outfit to do the job for you, I won't hold you to our agreement. Believe me."

"But Mr. Nolan, can't you fit the work in somehow between the other—"

"I'm sorry. Got to run. There's a lot going on here." Rachel heard lots of hammering and sawing in the background. Still, she doubted George Nolan was desperately needed by his work crew. The noise level did give him an easy out, though.

There was clearly nothing she could do. She promised to let him know if she still wanted him to do the work and said goodbye. Then she angrily hung up with phone, slamming it into the cradle.

She turned to her customer, still playing toss the dog with Charlie.

He glanced up at her, his dark eyes sympathetic and she knew he had overheard every word. "Bad news?"

Rachel shook her head. She hesitated answering him. It didn't seem professional to tell this customer her whole life story. What did he care about her contractor problems?

But his expression was so sympathetic and the look in his brown eyes willed her to just…vent.

"Yes, it was bad news. I hired a contractor to work on the cottage behind this house. It needs a new roof and there's water damage that needs repair. He was supposed to start last week and kept putting me off. Now he tells me he's backed up with another project and can't start for another month. I don't know if I can even find anyone now to do it before the winter. And he did have the lowest price. I really need to rent that space out. It's part of my plan."

"Your plan?"

"I was counting on the income to cover some expenses when I bought this place. Just until I get some momentum with the store."

"Oh, I see." Jack nodded with a thoughtful expression. "And where do you and Charlie live, upstairs?"

"That's right. There's an apartment on the upper floors." Rachel had that part of the building renovated before she moved in. The duplex was a very charming space, more than double the size of her apartment in the city.

Jack didn't say anything and Rachel felt suddenly self conscious. "I'm sorry. I didn't mean to bore you with all this stuff. I'll figure it out somehow."

He looked down at Charlie again. The baby smiled up at him and gurgled.

"Maybe I can help. I do that type of work myself."

"You do?" Rachel wasn't entirely surprised. She'd guessed he was in some blue collar job by the way he was dressed. If he could really take on this work, it would definitely be her lucky day.

"Could you take a look now and let me know what you think?"

He nodded. "Sure, lead the way."

Rachel picked up Charlie and grabbed her key ring from under the counter. She led Jack out a side door at the rear of the shop, which opened at the back of the porch, and then down a few steps to the gravel drive. They walked across the sloping lawn. Jack dipped his head as he passed beneath some trees. They looked like apple or cherry, but he couldn't be sure. He imagined they brightened the property in the spring, when they blossomed.

"It's pretty back here," he said.

"It's very quiet. And private. I'm going to make a big garden over there by the fence…if I ever get a chance."

He glanced at her and smiled. She had plans, this woman. He had to grant her that.

"I'm sure you will," he said.

They came to the cottage at the back of the property and Jack walked around it slowly, then climbed a ladder propped against the building. He examined the roof, pushing aside a blue tarpaulin that was covering the leaky patch. He felt around with his hands and pulled off a few rotten roof shingles.

Rachel stood back in the shade and watched him work. He'd shrugged off his sweatshirt at some point en route through her backyard and the thin black fabric of his T-shirt outlined every rippling muscle in his shoulders and back. Rachel knew she was staring—and drooling, just a little— but with his back turned, she allowed herself the tiny indulgence.

The cottage was as old as the house but far more run down. It hadn't been used for years but had loads of potential. Julia Martinelli, the Realtor who had sold Rachel the house, had promised that the space could bring in a very good rent once it was renovated. Rachel had bought the house, depending on the extra income to keep her financially afloat. Business so far had been promising, but she still wasn't making any profit. She didn't want to panic. But the truth was, she seemed to need the cottage income more and more each week.

Julia was the first person Rachel had met when she came

to town, nearly six months ago. She'd found Rachel the house, helped her set up her business and had quickly become one of Rachel's dearest friends, most trusted advisor and Charlie's favorite aunt. Rachel had never had a best friend like her before and she was sure she'd have made it this far in her new life without Julia's friendship and support. And her zany humor.

She couldn't wait to tell Julia about Jack Sawyer. It was going to be a two latte coffee break, at least.

Jack came down the ladder and brushed his hands together to rub off the dirt. "Not so bad. Let's see inside."

Cheered by his diagnosis, Rachel quickly headed for the front door. With Charlie in her arms, she handed Jack the key. He twisted it around a few times but the door wouldn't budge.

"Are sure this is the right one?"

"Here, let me try. It's pretty temperamental. You need to sort of twist and push down. Can you hold Charlie a minute?"

Jack looked surprised at the request, then quickly nodded. He held out his arms and Rachel handed the baby over. While she fiddled with the key, she couldn't help noticing the way Jack held Charlie, very carefully and gently, as if cradling an armload of Baccarat crystal. His face wore an amazingly tender expression, which didn't change one bit when Charlie started climbing up his chest and tugged at his hair.

Rachel gave the door the necessary twist and jiggle and it finally popped open.

"There we go," she said leading the way inside. "I know it doesn't look like much. I'd just like to fix it up enough so that I can rent it out. "

Jack carefully handed Charlie back, then walked in and looked around at the large, main room. "Okay, let's see what we have in here."

A small kitchen was built in one corner, separated from the rest of the lay-out by a snack bar. There was a wood-burning stove on one wall and a short hall that lead to a bedroom and bath.

After touring the layout he returned to the main room where she waited. "The walls and ceilings in the back rooms don't seem to have any damage. A fresh coat of paint back there should do it. This room, though, is pretty bad."

He stared up at the ceiling, then reached up to push at the tiles on the ceiling. Once again, she was treated to a view of his great body in action. Long lean legs and slim hips, broad shoulders and long, muscular arms. It had been awhile since she met a man so totally, blatantly attractive. If he really took this job, she'd have to see him every day. What a distraction that would be.

Did she really want that? She wasn't looking for a man in her life right now. That wasn't in her plan.

Get a grip, Rachel. A guy like that definitely has as girl-friend or a wife. Or some significant other lurking around.

He turned to her suddenly, and Rachel felt her face flush, as if he could read her thoughts.

"I have a few ideas about what we could do in here. Would you like to hear them?"

Rachel felt her mouth go dry and didn't answer at first. Charlie grabbed her earring, and she shifted him in her arms. "Sure. Go right ahead."

"I'd put a new roof on, of course. The building is so small, it's worth it to do the whole roof, not just a patch job. The renovation in here could be interesting…."

He picked up a scrap of paper and a pencil from the counter and sketched out the floor space. Then showed Rachel how he would remove the damaged ceiling tile and open the space to expose the rafters and make a vaulted ceiling, with a skylights in the main room and kitchen.

"Wow, that sounds great." Rachel looked up at him. "But what's that all going to cost? I think it might be too expensive," she said frankly.

"Well…let's see. What was the other contractor charging you?"

Rachel told him the figure, sure that this job would be at least double.

Jack looked down at his sketch again. "Sure, I could do it for that much."

"You could?" Rachel looked at him with disbelief. His ideas were the most creative she'd heard from any of the contractors she'd spoken to. George Nolan was reliable, but a real no-frills outfit. Jack Sawyer had a much more artistic perspective. How could his price be so low? Something wasn't quite right here.

"Are you sure that's a realistic price? I mean, there won't be any surprises for me later when I get the final bill?"

"I work on my own. I don't have a big crew to pay and a lot of overhead costs that larger outfits have to figure in. And I have some great cheap sources for my materials." Sensing that she wasn't totally convinced, he added, "And I need the work. The job I had lined up for this month just fell through. I could start in a day or so, and be done in a few weeks."

"Really?'

"Absolutely."

He suddenly looked a little anxious about her reply. She guessed he really did need the work. Then he smiled at her and met her gaze with his soft dark eyes. A reassuring look that said, *Trust me. I'm a nice guy.*

Rachel did want to trust him. Still, she'd learned better by now. Or hoped she had.

"I'll need references. And a written estimate and a contract," she said. "You're licensed and bonded, right?"

"Of course. I'll have the references for you tomorrow.... So, we have a deal?"

"Yes, it's a deal." Rachel extended her free hand. He looked surprised at first, then took it in his own. His grip was strong and warm. His touch was...distracting. He gazed down at her, a warm light dancing in his eyes.

By the time he'd let go of her hand, Rachel felt her pulse speeding double time.

Maybe this wasn't such a good idea after all, she thought. But beggars couldn't be choosers. His sudden appearance, just when found herself in a bind, seemed like a gift from the universe. She'd just have to get her hormones under control.

Maybe some speed walking in the early morning would help. She needed the exercise anyway to burn off the last of her baby weight.

He'd better not take his shirt off while he was working. Maybe she'd have to write that into their agreement.

"I just need to take some measurements in here for the estimate. I don't have my tool box with me, though. Can I use this?" He picked up a metal measuring tape and yard stick that had been left on the counter top.

"Of course. Help yourself. I'll wait for you outside, okay? It's a little stuffy in here."

"Sure. I won't be a minute." He smiled at her again and Rachel knew her need for fresh air didn't have anything to do with being in the cottage.

Rachel headed for the door, brushing disturbingly close in the small space before she stepped outside again.

Once outside she gulped in a few breaths of cool, fresh air, eager to clear her head. She stepped over to the cool shade and set Charlie down on the grass, then sat down beside him.

She was glad to have a moment on her own, to get herself together. It wasn't like her to get all rattled just because some hot guy smiled at her. She didn't like the feeling. Not at all.

He soon stepped out of the cottage and closed the door. Then he stood a moment looking at her and Charlie where they sat. A slow, warm smile spread over his face and Rachel felt completely undone again.

She scooped up Charlie, forcing a bland expression and hoped she wasn't blushing again.

Jack followed Rachel back into the store. She went behind the counter and then handed him a business card. "Here's my phone number, in case you need to call. Do you have a business card, Jack?"

"Sure…" He took out his wallet and flipped it open. Then suddenly flipped it closed. "I'm sorry… Looks like I'm all out. Here, let me jot down my cell number for you."

Rachel nodded, handing him a pen and paper. "I guess I'll see you tomorrow then."

"I'll be here around noon, is that okay?"

Rachel nodded. "Sure, that will be fine."

He'd said he was just passing through and now she wondered if he lived far away. Would he need to take a room someplace in order to be back here in the morning?

Well, that wasn't her problem. Considering her experience with George Nolan, she wondered if she'd really see Jack Sawyer again.

But something told her she would.

He was smiling down at Charlie again and lightly touched the little boy's hand. "So long, Charlie. I'll see you soon, okay? We can play that game again."

The tenderness in his tone caught Rachel's attention. She had to smile up at him when he finally looked her way. She realized she hadn't sold him anything from the store. But that didn't seem to matter.

"I'm glad you decided to drop in and look around," Rachel said with a laugh.

He nodded, but barely returned her smile. "So am I, Rachel."

Then he turned and left the store. The bell on the door rang as he walked out. Then suddenly, it seemed very quiet.

Rachel picked Charlie up out of his seat and held him in her arms. Her little boy looked drowsy and she wondered if she should try a nap again. Jack had given the baby quite a work-out with their dog tossing game.

There was something about Jack Sawyer. Rachel couldn't

put her finger on it. He was good looking. Smart. Even had a surprisingly kind side.

But still, there was something a little…off. That didn't quite fit.

She wondered if his references would check out. If they did, she'd hire him, of course. She'd never find anyone else to do the job at that price, or at this late date so close to winter. Besides…she did sort of like him. Even though she knew she shouldn't let herself.

Rachel rocked Charlie on her shoulder and slowly walked back to his nursery, humming "Rockin' Robin" again. She could hardly wait for him to fall asleep so she could call Julia.

Jack walked down to his car, slipped inside and drove down the quiet, shady street. By the time he'd reached the corner, he felt a strong impulse to pull a screeching U-turn, go back to Rachel Reilly and come clean with her completely.

Why did she have to be so damned beautiful?

Of all the mental images he'd had of his son's mother, he'd never expected her to be such a damned knockout. He'd expected anything but. He thought of her, standing in the buttery sunlight in her shop, with her soft, curly hair and creamy complexion, and those big hazel eyes. Her figure was curvy, a bit more voluptuous than the lean, slinky model types he usually dated. But those curves were amazingly enticing. He wondered now what he'd been missing.

She'd looked like an angel holding Charlie in her arms. Then later, sitting under the apple tree, she could have been posing for a softly hued painting by some romantic nineteenth century artist.

Why in the world did a woman who looked like that go to a sperm bank to get pregnant? She could have men waiting in line to bed her. The minute he'd set eyes on her, he'd felt like getting in line himself.

Wasn't this situation complicated enough?

It had been sheer madness to even suggest that he do the work on her cottage. He didn't know what had gotten into him. Of course he could do the work. It might even be fun. He'd worked his way through college on construction crews and wasn't afraid to get his hands dirty. He could easily come up with the references and credentials she wanted. That wasn't any problem either.

The problem was lying to her. She seemed a nice person. A reasonable person.

But of course, you never know. She might go berserk if she heard the donor dad of her child had searched for, and found, her and the baby. She might decide she'd never let him see him Charlie again.

When she'd stepped out of that back room carrying his son, Jack had thought for a second he was actually going to faint.

Jack had expected to feel moved by the sight of his son. But feeling his heart so full of love it was about to burst... well, that was a totally unexpected experience. And one previously unknown to him.

When she asked him to hold Charlie and he felt him so close, breathing right into his ear...his entire body was trembling. His son, his very own flesh and blood. In his arms for the first time.

He wasn't a man to break down crying. But this was different. This was the real thing.

Jack knew in an instant Charlie had forever sealed his fate. Forever marked his life's course. Charlie was his lodestar now, his touchstone.

He'd nearly lost it completely and told her everything.

But it hadn't been the right time. The right way to do it.

It was more important than ever to find out for sure if she was a good mother before he could determine his approach. Sure, she seemed nice. But first impressions could be deceiving.

Case in point. Look how he'd just deceived her.

Until he knew more about her, he couldn't jump to conclusions. And he certainly couldn't let his hormones distort his judgment. There was still a lot to find out.

But was planting himself on her property, disguised as some down-and-out handyman, the right way to go about this? Jack didn't think so. It wasn't ethical. Or fair.

Oh, who was he kidding? Sure, he wanted to find out about her. But it was the boy. His boy. The temptation of being near his son every day was hard to resist. Watching him play, laugh, sleep. Not just hard. Impossible.

Still, Jack wasn't sure if he should return to Rachel Reilly's store tomorrow, as he'd promised. He could just call and make some excuse to her. Or just disappear without any word of explanation.

Yet it was funny how that had all come together though, just at the moment of his visit. Jack wasn't a very spiritual man, yet this all seemed like some sort of gift from the universe. Should he really just pass on the opportunity?

Either way, whether he returned to work for her or disappeared into the blue, she would eventually find out who he was and why he'd come to visit today. Jack didn't even want to think far enough to imagine her reaction.

The entire situation presented as many problems as it solved. He almost regretted coming here and not taking the advice he'd been offered.

Almost, but not quite. Not at all, when he thought back to Charlie.

Jack didn't know for sure what he would do. Or should do.

He did know he was hungry, exhausted and this day of all days had shaken him to core.

At least he had all night to figure it out.

Chapter Two

"I love this place. I could live here. Honestly."

Julia Martinelli strolled around the shop, surveying the wares with a wistful sigh. No matter how many times Rachel's best pal dropped in at Pretty Baby—and she visited nearly every day—she always wore a look of wonder...and longing.

It was a short walk down Main Street to Pretty Baby from Home Sweet Home Realty. If Julia didn't come for a morning coffee break, she often brought lunch. Like today.

Rachel was hungry, but her stomach felt jumpy, too. Nerves about seeing Jack Sawyer again, though she hated to admit it. He said he'd come by noon and it was now about half past. That wasn't a good sign, she thought. But she didn't want to spin her wheels about it. If he came, he came. He did seem to be too good to be true...and maybe, he was.

Julia had wandered over to the infant wear. She picked up a pair of fuzzy pink knitted booties, stuck them on her fingers and wiggled them around like tiny feet.

"These are adorable? So sweet..." She sighed and put them back again. "Can't you please fix me a little room in the back, like Charlie's? I'll even pay rent."

"Sorry, I need the extra space for storage. But maybe you can rent out the cottage when it's fixed up. I'll even give you a discount."

The bright-eyed blonde glanced at Rachel, then sat down across from her at the counter. She opened the two bags she'd brought and began to spread out their lunch.

"Thanks, pal. I'll think about it. So, what's the story with the roof repairs? I'm sorry I wasn't able to call you back yesterday."

Rachel had called Julia soon after Charlie went down for his nap. But her friend had been busy with a client and was out last night on a date, so they'd never caught up.

"George Nolan left me hanging for a week, then bailed out on me totally. He said he was backed up on a bigger job and wouldn't get to the cottage for a month or more."

"You're kidding? That's the last time I recommend him for a job. I'll tell him myself, too. Here's your salad. And if that's too healthy for you, I also brought some chocolate chip cookies from the bakery."

"Thanks. This looks great." Rachel flipped the container lid and took a bite. Julia did the same.

"There must be someone besides George who could do it." Julia shrugged. She speared a hunk of lettuce with her plastic fork . "Do you need some more names to call?"

Rachel's well-connected pal knew just about every guy in town who owed a hammer or knew how to handle a paint brush. Without Julia's advice and recommendations, Rachel never would have been able to renovate her house and set up her shop in so short a time. But everyone on Julia's list for the roofing job had either been booked solid, not interested in such a small project, or asked too high a price.

"I found someone."

Julia squinted at her. "Already?"

Rachel nodded. She knew Julia was surprised that she'd managed that feat without her help. "He's even dropped off his estimate, references and a contract."

Rachel had found the thick manila envelope stuffing up the mail box when she'd opened the store that morning.

"He said he needs the work and I know he wants to start quickly. He's either efficient and responsible...or totally desperate."

"Maybe a little of both," Julia offered. "How did you find this guy again?"

"He just walked into the store. Yesterday afternoon. He was standing near the counter when I took the phone call from George, so he heard everything. We started talking and it turns out he does that type of work and is in between jobs. He looked at the cottage and had some really great ideas, too. He showed me how he could open up the ceiling to show the rafters and add skylights. That would really look nice, don't you think?"

"Definitely.... What's this guy's name? Maybe I know him."

"Jack Sawyer."

"Hmm...not ringing any bells." Julia sipped her coffee and Rachel couldn't tell what she was thinking. Probably that it wasn't wise to hire a guy who just walks in off the street, from out the blue. Even if he does have good ideas. "Is he from around here?"

"I'm not sure," Rachel said honestly. "I mean, I didn't ask. His letterhead has a local P.O. Box. But his references were all from Connecticut and New York."

Julia glanced at her, but didn't say anything. They both knew that could mean anything. Anyone could get a post office box.

She reached for a roll, unwrapped it and then broke off a small bite. Julia was a few years older and sometimes took on a protective attitude. Not in a bad way, though. It was just that Julia had lived in Blue Lake all her life, except for college, and was totally familiar with small-town ways. Which were mostly friendly and helpful...but sometimes not. Especially to someone considered an outsider.

"Can I see his card? Maybe I'll recognize the name of his company," Julia said.

"He didn't have a card handy." Rachel forced a small smile. That didn't sound very good either, did it? "But all of his paper work looked in order—the estimate, the contract. He gave me some references, too."

"Did you call them?"

Rachel nodded. "They all checked out fine. Glowing reports. Said he was reliable. Neat. Creative."

Julia shrugged. "Sounds like you caught a good one, Rachel."

"Right, let's hope."

She nearly blurted out that he was absolute eye candy. Though she didn't know yet if that was a plus or a minus.

Rachel had finished her salad, but hesitated reaching for the bakery bag of cookies. Wasn't she supposed to start a diet today, to take off the rest of her baby weight?

Funny how a few friendly smiles from a handsome guy could get you motivated about your appearance again. Rachel knew she'd even gone to a little more trouble getting dressed this morning. Jack Sawyer had caught her yesterday looking like a total mess.

She sighed and reached for the cookie bag. "How did it go with Gary? Did you have a good time?"

Julia fiddled with her fork, then tucked a strand of her golden hair behind her ear. "It was fine. We had very nice time. It was...nice."

"That bad, huh? I'm sorry," she said sincerely.

"Gary can be very funny. He makes me laugh. I mean, that's why I agreed to go out with him in the first place, you know?"

Rachel nodded. She knew Julia certainly had not starting seeing Gary Kramer because of his looks. He wasn't awful looking. Maybe even cute, in a geeky way. Just not the type of man she'd match with Julia, who was more than pretty. Gary looked every inch an accountant, which was still at least an inch or two shorter than her tall, leggy friend who was over five feet ten in heels. It wasn't just his looks. Rachel wasn't so superficial to judge people on those terms.

There was just something lacking about Gary, a passive quality maybe that didn't seem a match to Julia's vibrant personality.

It was a mystery to Rachel as to why Julia couldn't meet the right man and find a serious relationship. She was a tall, lithe blonde with a big blue eyes, intelligent, successful and the sweetest, most loyal soul in the world. If that wasn't enough, she was a great cook, too.

But just like so many single women their age, Julia was stuck on the dating treadmill, putting in a lot of time and effort, but getting nowhere. Julia had been married once, right after college to her high school sweetheart. If not for that choice, she may have never returned to Blue Lake. But now she was settled here, with a successful business, not to mention her sweet but flighty mother who needed Julia's level-headed supervision.

Julia thought she'd kissed just about every frog in this very small pond and still hadn't found her prince. All she wanted was to meet a nice man, get married and have a baby. Why was that so hard? Rachel thought it was so unfair that the happiness so many women found so easily seemed to constantly elude her friend. She never lacked for dates. But nothing ever lasted.

Rachel knew the feeling. She'd been through it all herself the last few years. Then she'd met Eric Rowland at a party and it seemed she'd finally met the perfect man. They'd gotten very serious very quickly and soon made plans to marry. But Eric had called off their wedding at the very last minute. Rachel was devastated and disillusioned.

After Eric, she didn't have the heart to start dating again and she'd lost all her trust in the opposite sex.

Rachel mourned the new life she had hoped to start with Eric. But one night, she decided she'd make a new life herself—rich, fulfilling, meaningful life with everything she ever wanted. Her own home, her own business and her own children. Without the help of any man.

She knew that Julia hadn't reached that point yet. But sometimes it seemed she was getting close.

"Are you going to see Gary again?" Rachel asked.

"Oh…I don't know. He said he would call. I usually have a three date rule. In Gary's case, I might reduce it to two." Julia sighed. "Maybe I should just do what you did, Rachel. Skip the husband all together and go straight for the baby."

Rachel would have laughed but Julia sounded so glum. She reached over and patted her friend's hand. "I'm not sure, Jules. Only you can answer that one. I will say that I just have this feeling the perfect guy is still out there waiting for you. I don't know why…I just do."

Julia smiled and rolled her eyes. "Oh, *please*. Now you sound like my *mother!*"

"Well, maybe for once, your mother is right." Rachel laughed and Julia rolled her eyes again. "What's Lucy up to? I haven't seen her in a few days. Has she married anyone this week?"

"Not that I know of. But I haven't checked my phone messages this morning."

Rachel loved Julia's mother; she was fun and full of life. She'd accepted and befriended Rachel and Charlie with no questions asked, and had even become Charlie's surrogate grandma.

But Lucy had this funny little habit of getting married. It had become the talk of the town.

In the small social circles of Blue Lake, Lucy Martinelli was known as "The Merry Widow." Though, technically speaking, only two of Lucy's four husbands had died. Husbands number two and four had been divorced. Which didn't bode well for Number Five. It seemed to Rachel the odd-numbered husbands had a very high mortality rate.

Julia seemed to be used to her mother's reputation, even found it amusing. But Rachel knew her mother's funny little habit worried Julia. They joked about Number Five, but Rachel wondered how Julia would really react if he ever materialized.

Knowing Lucy, it was more a question of when, rather than if.

"She actually is dating someone now. His name is Lester and of course, she claims it's true love. Again." Julia sighed and shook her head. "She did promise me they were going to take it very slowly though. I think she learned a lesson with Number Three."

"Number three?" Rachel had trouble keep Lucy's marriages straight.

"Roscoe Whiteburn, the guy she married in Vegas?"

"Oh...right. I remember now." Rachel nodded and grinned.

"Too bad for my Mom that husbands you marry in Vegas don't stay in Vegas," Julia said.

"If you ever get tired of real estate, your mother's romances would make a great TV movie."

"Don't think it didn't cross my mind. I'm waiting for a few more husbands. Did Henry the Eighth have seven wives or eight?"

"Six, actually," Rachel replied.

"Wow, she's really getting close now." Julia took a bite of her cookie, chewing with a thoughtful expression.

Rachel smiled and gathered up the trash from their lunches, then dumped it in the garbage. Julia whisked the crumbs off the counter top with her hand, then put on some fresh lipstick. Rachel could tell she was getting ready to return to her office.

Charlie had eaten earlier and was in the midst of his post-lunch snooze. She glanced at her watch and saw it was nearly one. Time to get him up soon.

"Well, back to work. I have to show the Wilcox's place at one-thirty. Joe Wilcox is so stubborn though, I'll never sell it. The place is a wreck and he won't budge a nickel on his price."

Rachel didn't envy Julia her work, dealing with difficult buyers and sellers all day and competing for sales with other brokers. Her friend made it look easy, though.

"I'm sure you'll work it out with him, Julia. We all know you could talk a dog off a meat wagon."

Julia grinned and picked up her bag. She knew it was true, but didn't like to flaunt her special talent. "Sincerity, kid. Once you can fake that, you've got it made."

Rachel was laughing when the bell on the shop door rang and Jack Sawyer walked in.

His gaze swept across the room and met her own. She struggled to mask her pleasure at seeing him. He smiled back in a way that seemed to say her struggle was in vain.

He walked towards her, wearing the same jeans and gray sweatshirt as yesterday, but with a white T-shirt underneath. Looking even better than yesterday, too. If possible.

She was surprised to see him. His cover note had said he'd call later, to see if she had any questions.

"I was in the area, so I thought I'd just drop by," he explained. "I hope I'm not interrupting anything?"

"No problem. We were just finishing lunch." Julia kicked her under the table. Rachel blinked, but showed no other reaction. "Jack, this is Julia Martinelli, a good friend of mine. She runs the real estate office down the street."

"Nice to meet you, Julia." Jack nodded at Julia and smiled politely.

"Hello, Jack. I hear you have big plans for the cottage."

His smile widened, attractive little lines fanning out at the corners of his dark eyes. "I'm not sure what you call big plans. I can put a new roof on and paint a few rooms."

"Which is just about all I can afford," Rachel added.

"Did you have a chance to look over the paperwork I left this morning?"

"Yes, I did. I called the references, too. Everything seems fine." Rachel picked up the folder with the signed contract and handed it to him.

"Great. The final cost might even be a little lower than the estimate." Jack shrugged. "I'll do my best to save you a few dollars if I can."

"I'm sure you will," Rachel glanced at Julia.

Was this guy too good to be true…or what?

Julia's answering look said, *What are you complaining about?*

"Well, I've got to run," Julia said, slipping on her sunglasses. "I'll call you later, okay?"

Rachel nodded, "Sure. Thanks for lunch."

"Anytime." Julia smiled at Jack as she walked past him on her way out. "Goodbye, Jack… See you."

He smiled back at her. "Nice to meet you."

When Julia reached the door, she slowly turned and caught Rachel's eye. She pressed her hand to her cheek, soundlessly mouthing the words, "He is so *hot!*"

Luckily, Jack stood with his back turned to the door, looking through the contents of the folder. Rachel blinked, forcing a blank expression when all she wanted to do was break out laughing.

He was hot.

Totally.

It wasn't just the subjective opinion of a woman who hadn't dated in nearly two years.

Once the shop door closed and Julia disappeared, Rachel

felt suddenly and utterly alone with him. She thought he'd have a few more words about the job and leave quickly, too. But he didn't seem in any hurry.

"Where's the little guy today?"

"Charlie? Oh, he's still having his afternoon siesta."

Jack nodded and smiled, a look of genuine tenderness in his eyes. "Tell him I said hello."

"I will," Rachel smiled back, thinking the remark had been sweet.

"How's business today?"

Rachel shrugged. "A little slow," she admitted. A look of concern flashed across his handsome face. Was he worried she wouldn't be able to pay him?

"But it's always slow on Wednesdays. I'm not sure why. It should pick up towards the weekend. People come to town for day trips—hiking, antique shopping, that sort of thing."

"And what do you do on the weekend, Rachel? Besides work, I mean?"

Rachel felt flustered. It wasn't so much the question as the way he was looking at her. Was he trying to find out if she had a boyfriend?

"Oh…nothing special. Spend time with Charlie, take him out to get fresh air, things like that."

He smiled, seeming quietly satisfied with her answer. "I guess it's not easy, running this business on your own and taking care of a little boy, too."

Rachel smiled and sighed. She didn't open up to strangers easily. Certainly not men. But there was something different about Jack. Something in his voice and the way he looked at her that broke through her natural reserve. He just seemed so…caring and sincere.

"It can feel overwhelming at times." She met his warm dark glance a moment, then looked away. "But I love my freedom. And I love Charlie even more. It's just the two of us, but that's fine with me. I wouldn't have it any other way."

"You sound very sure of that," he said quietly.

His reply made her realize just how she had sounded—as if she was warning him off. Warning him there wasn't any place in her life for anyone else. Like a man.

Well, there wasn't. So maybe that was a good thing. She smiled at him, noticing he didn't smile back.

"I am sure," she said evenly.

He gazed at her, his head tilted to one side.

"You know, Rachel, the one thing I've learned about life is…you can never be totally sure. Of anything. It pays to expect the unexpected. Know what I mean?"

Rachel didn't answer right away. Was he trying to tell her something? It seemed like he might be.

Then Rachel decided she was reading too much into the conversation. Perhaps he was just talking about his own life in a vague, general way.

Perhaps some surprising twist of fate had colored his philosophy. Maybe someday she'd find out what that was, but for now she was content to let it go.

Their friendly chat seemed suddenly too deep and serious.

"I'll remember that, Jack. But you do sound a little like a fortune cookie," she teased him.

"I had Chinese food for lunch." He slowly smiled and she realized he was teasing her back. "I'll be back to start the job on Friday. I need a day to square away some other business."

Two days? It seemed too long to wait to see him again.

Rachel forced an easy smile. "Sounds good. See you then."

"So long, Rachel." He turned and headed for the door. She tried to look away but couldn't take her eyes off him until he walked out of the shop.

The store seemed suddenly very quiet and empty. She turned on some classical music. Then stood at one of the display tables, folding baby sweaters. Unable to get Jack Sawyer's image out of her mind. He had an effect on her. Too great an effect. How was she going to manage several weeks of him working here? She had to get over this fast or she'd end up miserable.

Okay, he's attractive. And nice. But he must be involved with somebody, somewhere. Men like that aren't just running around, unclaimed.

If they are, there's a reason. Not a good one, either. You've found that out the hard way.

The bell above the shop door rang, interrupting her silent pep talk. Two attractive, well-dressed women walked in.

Snippets of overheard conversation told her they were out for the afternoon, having lunch, getting manicures, shopping. She half-envied them. Then she reminded herself that at the end of the day, she didn't have answer to anyone about what she did, where she'd gone, or what she'd spent.

Attractive men might come and go. As she'd just told Jack, she really did value her total and complete independence.

"Ladies? Can I help you with anything?" She walked over and greeted them.

"We're invited to a baby shower and the mother-to-be said she registered here. Could you look up her Wish List?"

"I'd be happy to. I'll print it out for you."

Rachel trotted back to the counter and took her place behind the laptop. Only a handful of "mothers-to-be" had registered at her shop. But she tried to give a good impression and act as if the place was very popular and there were hundreds.

Rachel's spirit suddenly lifted with the prospect of an easy sale. Or two. "Wish List" shoppers were her favorite, next to doting grandmothers. They rarely left the store without a shopping bag in hand.

Rachel was busy for the rest of the afternoon with more customers and catching up on phone calls. She locked the door at half past five and carried Charlie upstairs to their apartment, feeling weary, but content.

She'd made some good sales during the afternoon and the thought cheered her. She still had some savings from liquidating all her assets in the city, but she knew she couldn't run the business at a loss forever. She needed to make a profit soon, or she'd be in trouble.

Renting the cottage would help. She felt relieved it would be ready in a few weeks. Maybe even by the end of the month.

She wasn't sure where Jack Sawyer had come from, but he'd sure stepped through the door at just the right time.

Truth was, she could hardly wait to see him again.

Chapter Three

Rachel was not a morning person. But Charlie was. At least at this stage of his life.

It was barely light outside as she shuffled around the kitchen, still half asleep as her coffee brewed. She could already tell it was going to be one of those oddly warm September days that feel more like sticky mid-July.

Charlie was teething again and warm weather made him even more fretful. He sat in his high chair, bright-eyed and alert, jamming his little fist in his mouth and making the saddest little face.

Rachel handed him a frozen wash cloth and he grabbed it eagerly and began chewing away.

A loud sound outside made him jump and caught her attention as well. She thought at first it was the trash collectors and their noisy truck stopping by. Then she realized the sounds were coming from the back of her house.

She pushed aside the kitchen curtain. Jack Sawyer stood

at the back of a beat-up looking red pickup truck, pulling open the gate. Then he reached into the truck bed and begun unloading his supplies.

The jeans he wore today were even more worn and distressed than his last pair, clinging to his long lean legs and hips. He wore large work gloves and his tanned arms were bare, wrapped around a big black roll of tar paper that he tugged out of the truck. His biceps and shoulder muscles bulged, well defined beneath a white T-shirt.

Rachel felt a jolt at the sight of him. She knew she really ought to step away from the window, but she couldn't help herself.

"Good morning, libido. This is your wake-up call," an annoying little voice teased her.

She watched as he pushed the roll of tar paper toward the cottage, his whole body involved in the effort. Then suddenly he stopped and looked straight at her.

Rachel didn't know what to do and froze in place. She hadn't even thought he was aware of her. And here she was, standing there in her night gown, low cut and clinging, pretty much baring all.

He slowly stood to his full height, lifted his hand and waved. He couldn't see much from this distance could he?

From the oddly bemused smile on his face, she could tell that he could.

She jumped back and yanked the curtain closed, then covered her face with her hands.

Well, that was embarrassing.

What in the world had she been thinking?

She hadn't been thinking. That was just the problem.

There was something about this guy that short circuited the wiring in her brain. In her entire body, to be truthful about it.

For the past two days, he'd never been far from her thoughts. The image of his smile. The sound of his voice. The way his dark eyes lit up when he laughed.

Now he was back. For three weeks. Maybe more. She felt a tug in her stomach, a liquidy warm current of excitement racing through her veins.

She didn't know what was going on with her. It was just so silly. She was going to totally ignore this…this…*thing* she had for him. It was just ridiculous.

They might need to speak once in a while about the work. But it didn't have to go any further than that.

Not if she didn't want it to.

And you don't. Just remember that.

She pushed her long hair back from her cheek, poured herself a mug of coffee and took a long fortifying sip, hoping the caffeine would sober her up. Then she lifted Charlie out of his chair and carried him upstairs again. She placed him in his crib so she could shower and dress.

A long, cold shower seemed in order this morning.

Jack leaned forward on the ladder, ripping off the rotted shingles and tossing them onto a tarpaulin on the ground. He'd started the job with a rush of adrenaline, inspired by the sight of his scantily clad employer. But that burst of energy had faded by now.

God, she looked gorgeous in the morning, her hair floating down around her bare shoulders and that half sleepy look on her face. For a while, all he could think about was dragging her off to bed.

But he was here to find out what kind of person she was, not how good she was in bed, he reminded himself.

It was hot out here today. And it wasn't just his fantasies turning up the temperature. He'd forgotten what it was like to work outdoors. He hadn't done this type of hands-on construction work since college. He considered himself fit, but trotting on a treadmill in a cushy health club was a far cry from this type of back-breaking labor.

What was he doing here anyway? Why wasn't he back in

New York, sitting in his air-conditioned office? He'd spent the entire day and night there yesterday, squaring things away so he could take off on this harebrained adventure. Of course, he hadn't told a soul what he was really up to. He could barely explain it to himself. He'd told his staff he was going on vacation—an unexpected, prolonged vacation, and didn't want to be bothered unless it was a dire emergency. Fat chance that would happen. He'd bet there were at least 50 messages piled up by now on his BlackBerry.

He had to be insane for even trying.

What had ever made him think this scheme was a good idea? *Patience. You've only been here three hours.*

It was going to take longer than that to find out what he wanted to know. She was pretty sharp. He didn't want to come on too strong either and make her suspicious. Fixing this roof was a slow, step-by-step process and that went double for getting to know her—and his child. It was going to take time and patience. Too bad he wasn't normally the patient type.

Jack wiped the sweat off his brow with the back of his hand and focused on the roof again, fueled by his frustration—including the spurt generated earlier that morning by the vision of Rachel at the window.

Immersed in the rhythm of his work, he barely noticed the sound of the screen door at the back of the house open and slam.

He definitely noticed Rachel strolling across the back yard with Charlie in her arms. She had on a dark blue sun dress with thin straps holding up the top and a long flowing skirt. Her long curly hair was swept up in a loose knot, at the back of her head. The entire effect was almost as bad as the nightgown and he was glad to be up on the ladder, where she couldn't see his immediate reaction.

She stood a short distance away, looking up at him, her hand cupped over her eyes to shade the sun. He pretended for a moment he didn't notice her there.

"Jack? How are you doing?"

Finally he stopped working and looked down at her. "It's coming along. This is the slowest part."

Especially if you haven't climbed a ladder and gotten your hands dirty for the last fifteen years.

Charlie waved at him and blurted out some baby gibberish. Jack waved back. He couldn't help but smile. He couldn't help coming down the ladder either to see his boy.

His boy.

If only he could reach out and take him in his arms. Just like that. It felt like the most perfectly natural thing to do in the world.

But of course, he didn't dare.

Rachel held out a big frosty bottle of water. "Want a drink? It's hot out here."

"Thanks. That was thoughtful." He gratefully took the water bottle and twisted off the top. He'd brought along some cold drinks in the truck, but they weren't nearly enough.

It was a small gesture. But some people wouldn't have gone to the trouble. She was considerate. He'd have to note that.

Maybe you should start a notebook. List all the good qualities you observe about her?… And all the bad.

In case there's ever a lawsuit or anything like that.

He glanced over and met her soft blue gaze. She smiled at him, looking pleased that he was enjoying the cold drink.

She didn't have any bad qualities. Not that he could see so far.

That should have been good news…but in a way, it also seemed a problem.

Charlie wiggled and she shifted him to her other arm. "It's hot out here today."

"Is it ever. I'm glad I didn't start this job in July."

"It should cool down by the end of the week. The weatherman says anyway."

"Hope so." He looked at her, then back at Charlie again. "How's the little man today? Does the heat bother him?"

"The shop is air conditioned, so he's comfortable inside. But he's teething right now and that's not much fun."

Teething? That must feel like a giant toothache. *And I think I have it tough today.*

"Does it hurt him much?"

"Sometimes I think it does. I give him something cold to rub on his gums…or a little medication." She shrugged. "Just one of those stages babies go through. And mothers."

And fathers, he wanted to add. Now he was one, too, and felt sorry for his little boy feeling any pain at all.

All he could do was let out a long sigh and look down longingly at his son. "I hope he feels better soon," he said finally.

"Thanks…I'm sure he will." Rachel looked down at Charlie with a loving expression and stroked back his soft hair with her hand.

She was a good mother. Caring, but also calm. That was important, Jack thought.

When Rachel looked back at him, she had an odd expression on her face. He'd shown too much, he realized. But it was too late.

He tugged his work gloves on and headed back up the ladder. "Better get back to it."

"I've got to get back to the shop. Let me know if you'd like some more water…or anything."

"Thanks." He was up about midway up the rungs and didn't even glance down when he answered.

He waited a moment, then finally watched her walk back to the house. With Charlie balanced on one side, her hips gently swayed under the tiered skirt, the soft line of her cheek and profile as she smiled, nuzzling Charlie's hair with her lips.

He felt a tug, as if an invisible string attached somewhere around his heart was reeling out to Charlie. And to her.

It wasn't the volcanic rush of heat he'd felt this morning

after spotting her at the window. This was different. Not a feeling generated below his belt but much higher, somewhere around his heart.

He wasn't used to that. It was downright...frightening.

Jack turned away and scoffed at himself. Then, practically hopped the rest of the way to the top of the ladder.

It was the baby. Stirring up all kinds of romantic fantasies about the mother. That's all it was. *Get a grip, pal,* he coached himself.

That sort of thing pushed his buttons. He knew it, as well as anybody. He'd been given up by his own mother when he'd been five years old. At an age when he could still vaguely remember her. Making it all the more traumatic.

You need to find out about her. Not fall for her, he reminded himself.

He yanked off another chunk of rotted roof shingles.

Just like this repair job, it all seemed much easier said than done.

Rachel entered the shop and sighed with relief at the cool blast of air that greeted her. She flipped the sign on the door back to "Welcome!" and set Charlie in his play pen, surrounded by soft blocks and pop-up toys.

Well, that was that.

She'd completed her visit to Jack for the day. Even brought him some water. She wouldn't go out to speak to him again. She wouldn't spare the guy another thought.

That was her plan and she was sticking to it.

The sound of him ferociously ripping apart the roof seemed to taunt her. She thought of the way he'd looked at Charlie, concerned to hear about the teething troubles. He was so...empathetic. Surprising in a guy like that. In any guy, actually.

Maybe he had children of his own somewhere. He hadn't mentioned it, but that didn't mean anything.

She turned on some music and pushed the volume up. A

jazz station today. But she could still hear him. Which made her think of him, which wasn't good.

She went to the store's front window, climbed inside and began pulling everything out. She would make a new display with an autumn theme. She'd been meaning to change the window all week, before the leaf peepers and "pick your own pumpkin" crowds hit town. She'd made some beautiful baby-sized Halloween costumes and wanted to show them off, hoping for orders.

The project was the perfect distraction for today. The perfect reminder that her life was way too busy right now for a man.

By the time five-thirty rolled around, Rachel found she'd stuck to at least half her plan. She'd changed the window and kept herself busy in the shop. She had not gone out to talk to Jack again—though she hadn't been able rid her thoughts of him completely.

Putting Charlie down for his afternoon nap at about three, she'd realized it was very quiet outside. She'd glanced out the window to spot Jack sprawled on his back under a tree.

He'd taken off his T-shirt and his muscular arms were folded up to shield his eyes from the sun. His broad, bare chest was ridged with well-defined muscles, covered with dark hair. His stomach was incredibly flat and hard-looking, entirely exposed by his low riding jeans.

The thought did occur, that as his employer, she should have been annoyed—or at least questioning—finding him that way in the middle of a work day. But the sight of him made her mouth go instantly dry, her knees turning to jelly.

She snapped the shade in Charlie's room down and instead of giving the baby his frozen wash cloth to teeth on, she pressed it to her flushed face.

Customers in the afternoon kept her very busy. She hadn't even noticed that it was nearly five-thirty…or that the noise behind the shop had stopped, until Jack walked in.

Rachel was handing a customer a package and giving change. She glanced at him. He stood at the door with his arms folded over his chest. He looked hot and tired, she thought. She tried hard not to think about the way he'd looked earlier that afternoon, laying under the tree without his shirt on. But it wasn't easy.

Luckily, he didn't seem in the mood to make conversation.

He didn't even come very far into the store but spoke to her standing in front of the door.

"Sorry to bother you, but I'm ready to go and your SUV is blocking my truck."

"Oh…sorry." She'd gone out for a few minutes during the day to pick up some diapers and hadn't even thought of parking behind the truck.

Rachel grabbed her car keys, which were under the counter and walked toward him.

"I can move it for you, just give me the keys."

"No, that's okay. I'll do it." Rachel glanced at him.

Why did he have to be so nice all the time? So helpful? That was part of the problem right there. She wasn't used to anyone always offering to help her do…anything. Somehow the attention made her uncomfortable.

He opened the door and let her walk out ahead, then followed. She climbed into the SUV and he walked up to his truck.

Rachel started the engine, put the vehicle in Reverse and began backing out the driveway.

A thump-thump sound and her car shaking crazily made her immediately hit the brake and put the car in Park again.

She jumped out and ran up to Jack, who was now sitting in his truck with all the windows open.

"Something's wrong with my car. It's making a funny sound."

He was wearing dark glasses that covered a good part of his face. But she could still tell he was not happy to hear it.

"Let me take a look," he said wearily.

He jumped out of the truck and walked back to her vehicle. He looked over the front and then walked to the back. Rachel followed him.

"You've got a flat. In the back on the right." He crouched down and took a closer look. "Looks like you drove over a nail or something. Didn't you notice anything odd when you drove it today?"

Rachel shrugged. "I guess not. Or I would have gone to a gas station."

She wasn't good with cars. When she heard a noise, she tended to turn up the radio and hope it would go away.

"Don't worry, I can fix it." She had changed a flat tire or two. Though not on this SUV, which was bigger by far then her other cars. But if it was too challenging, she'd call somebody.

Jack stood up and brushed his hands together. "I'll do it for you." The spare was secured to the tail gate, at the back of the tail gate. Jack felt the air pressure with his hand. "Where's the jack and all the stuff, in back?"

"Thanks, but you really don't have to do this."

"It won't take long. I don't want to leave you here tonight without a car in working order. What if something happens with Charlie and you need to bring him to an emergency room?"

"I guess I'd call a neighbor…or 911 if it was that serious," she answered honestly.

Once again, his thoughtful streak surprised her. He certainly hadn't seemed the nurturing type when she first met him. More of a hunk, handyman, drifter. But you never know….

"Just give me the keys, Rachel. I can take care of it in a few minutes. Besides, you're still blocking my truck. Either I fix it, or I sleep over."

He looked at her, checking her reaction. His tone was serious, but a light in his dark eyes told her he was teasing.

Rachel didn't dare reply. She forced a blank expression and handed him the keys.

"I'd better get back inside and check on Charlie."

"I'll let you know when I'm done."

He clicked open the tailgate and immediately got to work.

Rachel went into the house through the side door, closed it, then leaned back against it and took a deep calming breath.

He was only teasing her. He was the type who said provocative things just to watch the way a woman would react. And she was such an easy mark. He must be having loads of fun.

Don't take him seriously, Rachel. You'll regret it…

With Charlie in his high chair, Rachel slipped on an apron and began preparing dinner. Charlie was still eating baby food, cereal and fruit mostly. Most nights, she just winged it for herself.

That was another thing she liked about living alone. If she wanted to cook scrambled eggs and toast three times a day for a week, there was no one to complain about the menu.

Tonight she'd planned to make a real meal. Pasta and meat sauce that was left over from entertaining Julia last weekend. Charlie liked spaghetti. He liked playing with it, mostly. She enjoyed watching him discover "real" food lately.

When Jack came up to the apartment, about half an hour later, dinner was just about done. He tapped on the door and she went to answer it.

"Here are your keys. I put the spare on and left the bad tire in the trunk. You need to drop it off at a gas station somewhere. I think it can be fixed."

"Thanks, Jack. I really appreciate your help. I'm sure you must be exhausted."

He shrugged. "I'm okay. Looking forward to a hot shower later," he admitted. He smiled at her and their eyes met. Rachel couldn't quite look away and felt suddenly at a loss for words.

"Mind if I wash my hands?"

"Oh…sure…come right in," She stepped aside and he walked to the kitchen sink. Rachel handed him a bottle of soap, then stepped back.

"Ya-ya-ya!" Charlie smacked the table of his high chair, seeming very excited to see Jack.

Jack turned to the baby and smiled over one broad shoulder.

"Hey, pal. How are you doing? Feeling better I see."

Charlie squealed and smacked the high chair table again.

Jack laughed. "I think he remembers me."

"Maybe." Rachel agreed. "He's also hungry for dinner. That's the way he calls for the waitress."

Jack tore some paper towel off the roll near the sink and wiped his hands. "Smells good. I don't blame him."

Rachel glanced at him quickly, then stepped over the stove and checked the boiling pasta. "Would you like to stay? It's nothing special. Just pasta and meatballs," she added.

Oh, God! What in heaven's name had made her say that?

She'd practically locked herself inside the store today, trying to avoid him. Now she'd invited him for dinner.

He seemed almost as surprised as she was. He leaned back on the counter and looked at her.

"Sounds good… If you're sure it's not too much trouble?"

"It's no trouble. I made more than enough. I can never judge amounts." She turned and glanced at him. "Consider it a thank-you for changing the tire."

She felt better finding this excuse. But she did owe him one for the favor. They both knew she could have backed the car into the street—flat and all. Despite his dire prediction of being stranded overnight.

"I'd be very pleased to stay. Thanks for the invitation."

She smiled at him, but didn't reply. "Everything's ready. I just need to set the table."

"I can do that. Where do you keep the dishes and silverware?"

Rachel was about to brush off his offer, then caught herself. Maybe, once in a while, it was okay to let a someone help her. Even a man. Even an attractive man, like Jack. It didn't have to threaten her entire existence and identity.

Jack Sawyer was no threat. He was just a nice guy who had for some strange reason, happened to come into her life.

Was there anything so wrong with that?

A short time later, they sat at the round oak kitchen table, Jack on one side and Rachel on the other, with Charlie in his high chair in between.

Rachel had whipped up a green salad and also found some Italian bread in the freezer that quickly crisped in the oven. She tugged out a bottle of red wine from the back of a cabinet, which seemed to add a little style to the humble offerings.

Jack had set the table neatly with all the necessary equipment and she added two antique wine glasses and a small vase of late blooming roses she'd cut yesterday from her front garden.

The table looked pleasing, definitely more inviting than it did when she ate alone. The last of the day's sunlight streamed through the windows, lending the cozy kitchen a honey glow.

It felt odd at first, eating dinner with someone in her house. Rachel was so accustomed to being alone with Charlie. But Jack was easy to be around. He didn't seem uncomfortable with silence, like most people she knew.

Including her former fiancé Eric, who had always been expressing himself, his feelings and opinions. His likes and dislikes. His verbal abilities were an asset as an attorney, Rachel supposed. But he couldn't seem to turn it off out of the office or courtroom. Another reason she'd been lucky he'd broken their engagement. She had to add that one to the list.

"This is delicious," Jack dabbed his mouth with a paper napkin. "You're a good cook."

"My repertoire is limited. But I have my moments," Rachel said.

"I can barely zap a microwave meal, so a home cooked dinner like this is a rare treat."

That was true, too. Cooking was not a trait often found in

the women he dated. What he neglected to mention was that most of his dining took place in restaurants with a lavish decor and an overpriced menu.

"Charlie seems to like his spaghetti," Jack leaned across and gently wiped a piece of spaghetti stuck to Charlie's cheek.

"He's just starting on regular food. He mostly likes to play with it."

"I can see that," Jack's smile widened as Charlie took another fistful of pasta and stuck it on top of his head. "Very creative, too."

Rachel smiled but was surprised again at Jack's attentions to her baby. Most men she'd met lately were ready to run the other way once they found out about Charlie. Oh, they'd say he was cute and ruffle his hair. But she knew they were secretly looking for the nearest exit.

Not that I'm in the market for a man, she reminded herself. It's just an interesting comparison.

Jack leaned over and wiped the spaghetti off Charlie's head, then tickled him under the chin, making the baby laugh.

"What's his favorite?"

"Bananas. He can eat a bunch by himself. I bet he'll be awesome on the monkey bars once he gets to school."

Jack glanced at her, a funny look flashing in his eyes.

"I bet he will be, too. But that's a long ways off."

"It goes by faster than you think."

"Very fast. I can see I've missed a lot," he said wistfully.

Rachel didn't quite get his meaning. Did he mean he'd missed a lot by not having children of his own?

"Do you have any children, Jack?"

He turned. The look on his face said she'd touched a nerve. "No, I don't. Why do you ask?"

"You're so good with kids. So…interested. You seem like you have some experience with children. Caring for them, I mean."

"I have a younger brother. I took care of him a lot while we were growing up."

Rachel could see that. He had a distinctly protective nature. "Your mother must have appreciated that."

Jack shrugged. "She wasn't around to thank me. She dumped us into foster care when I was about five and he was just a baby. We were moved to a lot of different families. But we were lucky we were never split up."

Jack reported this trauma in a flat, unfeeling voice. He had turned away from her again to play with Charlie, offering his hand for the baby to slap with a spoon.

Rachel felt a jolt at his admission. "That's very sad. I'm sorry," she said quietly. "Where's your brother now? Are you still in close touch with him?"

Jack glanced at her. "He's in California. A big-shot entertainment lawyer. He's done well for himself, considering where we started."

Then he realized how that looked to her. As if he hadn't done well for himself. And was even making an excuse.

The truth was that he was even more successful and even wealthier than his kid brother. But to Rachel it had to look as if he was the slacker, the black sheep.

"You sound proud of him."

"I am," Jack said honestly. Then to cover his tracks, he quickly added, "I don't begrudge Brian his success. He earned it. I found a job in construction right after high school and took to the life, moving around a lot. Not having to answer to anyone."

He did like to travel and did like being his own boss.

But still felt a guilty twinge leaving out the scholarships to college and graduate school. His achievements as an architect and professional life.

"So, you like your freedom," she said with a smile.

"I do." He nodded and sipped his wine.

Rachel understood that, too. But it also warned her that

Jack was, in some ways, just as she'd guessed. A drifter, living out of the back of his truck, unlikely to make any long-term commitments.

Just as well to get that out on the table right up front. That will keep me from getting any insane ideas about him.

"Mind if I ask you a personal question?"

She did mind, but felt it was only fair to let him have one free shot. She could guess what was coming.

"Where's Charlie's father? Isn't that it?"

One dark brow rose curiously. "Well...that is a good question."

Rachel sighed. She wanted to answer him with the truth. The complete truth. For some reason, she felt she could tell this man everything.

But maybe that was just the wine. Some distant, foggy part of her brain warned she'd better be careful. And not nearly so trusting.

"I never really knew Charlie's father. He didn't want anything to do with me. That was always...the arrangement."

She spoke quickly, not even glancing at Jack as she spoke. Okay, it wasn't the complete truth. But not really a lie either, she reflected.

Finally, she looked back at him, not knowing what his reaction would be. The look in his dark brown eyes was sympathetic. Accepting. She could tell he didn't judge her... which was refreshing.

His expression was also solemn...and uneasy.

Why should he be uneasy? She was the one baring her darkest secrets. But maybe any kind of really personal exchange made him nervous. The distant type.

The next thing he said confirmed her suspicion.

"You don't have to say more, Rachel. I shouldn't have asked."

"You didn't," she reminded him. "I just expected you were about to. I was right, wasn't I?"

He shook his head. "No, not at all... I was going to ask if

you had any family around here, any sisters or brothers to help you with Charlie."

"I have one sister," she offered. "We're not very close. Especially since our mother died. Nora has never seen Charlie."

"Really? Does she live far away?"

"Not at all. Just down in New York." Rachel's voice trailed off. The real reason for their estrangement seemed too personal to confide. Nora disapproved of Rachel choosing to be a single mother and fathering her child through a sperm bank.

"We're just very different. We always were. Nora is very... conservative. Logical and practical. I've was always the creative, impractical one."

"I see." Jack smiled. "I'm glad I met the impractical sister. Nora probably would have never hired me so quickly."

"No, she probably wouldn't have," Rachel agreed with a laugh.

Charlie fussed restlessly in his chair. Rachel rose and took him in her arms.

"Time for a bath, little man." She said nuzzling him. "We need to wash that spaghetti out of your hair."

Jack watched her, a soft look coming over his strong features.

"Does he have a bath every night?"

"Every single. Sometimes during the middle of the day, too. Depending on what he's gotten into."

Jack got up from the table and started gathering the dirty dishes. "Guess I'd better get going. It's getting late."

She was surprised at his sudden need to leave. But maybe it was best.

"Don't bother with the dishes. I'll do that later," she said.

"It's okay. I don't want to leave you with a big mess."

He'd already carried one pile dishes to the sink, now came back for what remained. He glanced up at her. "Go ahead, start his bath. I'll be done in a minute."

Rachel was going to argue with him more, then decided not to. He's seemed determined to help her.

Maybe it has something to do with losing his own mother at such a young age.

Well, she wasn't a psychiatrist. She'd never really know. It did seem an unusual and refreshing trait to find in a single guy her age.

She went upstairs to the apartment's second floor, where there was a bathroom with a claw foot tub and bedrooms for herself and Charlie. Holding Charlie tight, she crouched down and started the tub water running. Then she carried him into his bedroom where she undressed him.

Rachel carried Charlie back to the bathroom, tested the water with her hand, then set him down in the tub in his special bath seat.

He flapped his hands on the top of the water and splashed, making the usual excited sounds while she tried to wash him up.

When she finally noticed Jack standing the doorway, she wasn't sure how long he'd been there.

"He seems to really like it," Jack said with a small smile.

"He likes playing with the water. Wait until I have to wash his hair. That's a different story.... Could you hand me that bottle of shampoo?"

Jack moved quickly and grabbed the bottle. "This one?"

"Thanks."

Charlie's head was already wet. Rachel squirted on the baby shampoo and lathered him up. As usual, he began to cry once she started to rinse off the suds.

Jack looked concerned. "Is the soap in his eyes?"

"It's the no tears kind. He just doesn't like water dumped on his head."

"I don't blame him...are you done yet?" Jack's sympathy was out of proportion, but touching at the same time.

Finally the nightly ordeal was over. Charlie was clean,

head to toe. Rachel lifted him out of the water as he clutched a rubber frog. She made a reach for his towel with one hand, but Jack was there first and carefully wrapped it around the baby, so he was snug and warm.

Charlie rested his head on Rachel's shoulder, his big brown eyes following Jack. "He looks sleepy."

"Finally." Rachel laughed quietly.

She carried Charlie into bedroom, which she'd left dimly lit. Jack followed and silently handed her things as she put on a fresh diaper and then put Charlie in his pajamas.

By the time he was ready for bed, her little boy was half asleep and felt heavy in her arms when she lifted him off the changing table.

She rocked him a moment, then laid him down in the crib. "Oh…the white dog. He can't fall asleep without it. I think I left it on the changing table…"

"Got it," Jack said with quiet triumph. He stepped back to the crib and nestled the stuffed toy beside Charlie's smooth cheek.

"He's a beautiful child," Jack whispered.

Rachel didn't answer. She didn't want to break the spell.

As they stood side by side, gazing down at the sleeping baby, she suddenly felt an amazing pull of closeness, intimacy.

This is what it would be like if Charlie had a father.

It would be good to share this beautiful boy with someone who loved him as much as I do. With someone who loved me, too.

But Jack was a stranger. He liked Charlie. But he didn't love him.

Her fantasies—and loneliness—were getting the best of her.

Jack slowly turned toward her. The way he looked into her eyes, she felt as if he could read her mind. His hands rose and gently touched her hair, then cupped her shoulders. She didn't mean to turn towards him as he willed, but she did.

He stared down at her a moment, then stepped even closer. She lifted her hand to his chest, as if to push him away, but was overcome by a different impulse entirely as she felt his heat and his heartbeat.

If there was a time to step back, this was it.

But she couldn't move a muscle.

He bent his head and his lips touched hers, testing at first, then with more intensity as he pulled her closer. Her arms slipped around his strong shoulders with a will all their own.

This couldn't be happening...but it was.

Really was.

Rachel felt herself melting against the contours of his hard, strong body, swept away on a wave of sensation. His firm, commanding mouth moved against hers, tasting, savoring, giving and taking. One strong hand glided down her back and the other, moved into her thick hair.

When was the last time she'd been kissed like this? Rachel asked herself.

Try...never, a small, distant voice answered.

Rachel wasn't sure how long they stood there, entwined in each other's arms. She wasn't sure what would have happened next if Charlie hadn't given out a soft cry.

Jack drew away and looked down into the crib.

"He's all right. Just having a dream, I guess." Rachel leaned over and checked the baby.

She briefly rested her hand on Charlie's back, then stood up and pushed her thick curly hair back from her face. She didn't know what to say.

She wanted to be annoyed at herself for letting it happen. But she honestly was not. She didn't think he felt the same. Reading the look on his face, she wondered if he was sorry now he'd kissed her.

"I'd better get going," Jack said quietly. He walked out into the hallway and she followed. "Thanks again for dinner."

"Thanks for fixing the flat."

"Right." He nodded and started to go. Then paused and met her gaze.

She had the distinct feeling he wanted to say something to her. Something serious.

Finally, he said, "Well...good night."

Just as well. She didn't want to hear him apologize after delivering the most awesome kiss of her life.

I'd see you out, Jack. But my toes are still curled.

"You can let yourself out the side door. It will lock behind you," she said instead.

"Okay, I will."

She walked to the railing and watched him disappear down the stairs.

"See you tomorrow," she called after him.

He didn't answer.

For some strange reason, she got the distinct feeling he couldn't leave fast enough.

Chapter Four

"Let me get this straight. He fixed a flat tire, cleaned up the kitchen after dinner and helped you give the baby a bath." Julia counted off Jack's accomplishments on her fingers.

"I wouldn't say he helped with the bath. He handed me the shampoo and a towel," Rachel corrected.

"Whatever. Then there was a 'mind blowing'—your words, not mine—kiss… And you have a problem with this?"

Hearing Julia retell the story, Rachel realized she did sound…irrational.

Rachel sipped her tall latte. It was not quite eight-thirty in the morning. Rachel had left a message on Julia's machine late last night saying she needed advice about a problem with Jack. Julia had rushed over first thing, to see why Rachel had sounded so unnerved.

"Listen, I know I sound a little nutty. But do you really think it's such a great idea to get involved with someone who works for me? Someone I barely know anything about?"

"Didn't you get to know him a little better last night? Sounds like he was hanging around for awhile. What did you talk about all that time?"

Rachel shrugged. "The usual stuff. He told me he grew up in foster homes. His mother abandoned him and his younger brother when Jack was only five years old."

"Wow, that's sad."

"Yes…it is, isn't it? I think it's affected him. Made him sort of a drifter. Afraid of being tied down." Julia didn't say anything, but her doubtful look spoke volumes. "He was talking about his work, doing construction. He said he likes his freedom. He likes to move around. You've dated more than I have, Julia. Don't you think he was trying to tell me something?"

"Okay, we can both translate the Man-Speak. But most guys do fly that flag at the start, Rachel. 'I'm a lone wolf, wandering the world. Tie me down and I'll die…' It's sort of a defensive maneuver."

"I think he means it. Oh, he might be interested in an affair. Maybe he has affairs all the time with women he works for," she added. The very thought that had irked and haunted her last night. "But he lets them know up front it won't lead to anything."

Julia smiled. "As I said before, what's the problem? What would be the harm if you did have an affair with him?" Julia countered. "Let's be honest, Rachel. I think you're still not over Eric and the way he dumped you. Jack is the perfect solution. He'll make you forget all about that creepy fiancé and make you feel great about yourself again. You don't want a heavy relationship right now? How about a superficial one? It won't be too serious, won't be demanding more than you want to give."

Recalling her response to Jack's single, smouldering kiss, Rachel thought she was ready to give Jack anything he asked of her and more. But she wouldn't admit that to Julia. It would just add fuel to her silly ideas.

"Julia, please? I just want a little advice on how to handle this. I need to let him know I'm not interested."

"Despite the way you acted last night, you mean?" Julia chided her.

Rachel sighed. "That was…a fluke. I got carried away. We were drinking red wine. It always goes to my head."

"Okay. If you say so." Julia shook her head. She reached across the table and patted Rachel's hand. "I don't mean to tease you. But guys that look like that—and wash dishes— don't come along every day."

"It's just bad timing…I'm not really the fling type," she added.

After one tiny taste of Jack's company, Rachel knew she could never get half-way involved with him. It would have to be an all-or-nothing for her.

"Listen, you don't have to make a big thing about it," Julia said, finally taking her seriously. "If he brings it up, just be honest. Say you like him, but you're not into dating right now. Or just say you don't want to get involved with someone who works for you." Julia sipped her coffee. She glanced at Rachel over the edge of her cup. "Keep it short and sweet. Most people tend to say way too much in those situations. That's what makes it feel awkward."

Rachel knew that was true enough. She was always the over-explaining type.

"Okay. Short and sweet. I know I gave completely different signals, Jack…but I really don't want to get romantically involved with you. Or even jump into bed. Nothing personal. Thanks for your interest."

Julia nodded. "Something like that."

Then they both laughed. Rachel felt better. As usual, talking it over with Julia put in perspective. She hadn't been out dating for a while. That was the reason a simple kiss had seemed so…momentous.

Okay, it had been more than a simple kiss.

But nonetheless, no need to get so bent out of shape over it. She could handle Jack, whatever his expectations were right now. Julia had helped her realize that.

So why did she nearly jump out of her skin when she heard his truck pull up the driveway?

Julia had heard it too. She glanced at Rachel but didn't say anything.

"He's here," Rachel practically whispered. She couldn't help it.

Julia gathered up her purse and briefcase and paper cup of coffee. "Just relax. Remember, keep it simple."

Rachel followed her as she walked to the door. She wasn't quite ready to see Julia go. As if her friend's presence could somehow protect her from having to face Jack.

"Okay. Thanks. I'll be fine."

Julia gazed her wistfully. "I'll keep my cell on if you need to get in touch."

"Thanks. You're a pal." Rachel gave her a quick hug and Julia walked out the door.

Behind the house, she heard Jack unloading building supplies from his truck. She watched from the window of Charlie's playroom.

Jack seemed intent on his work and didn't even glance at the house. He seemed anxious to get started. She watched as he set up the ladder, climb up and begin working where he'd left off the day before.

It looked like she'd have to wait to find out if he was intent on picking up with her where they'd left off last night.

Saturday was the shop's busiest day of the week. She had thought about hiring an extra sales person for Saturdays. But so far, she still couldn't afford it.

She did her best to keep everyone happy, running from one side of the store the other, trying to be cheerful, and helpful... and apologetic when it seemed customers were losing patience as they waited for attention.

She didn't have too much free time to fret about Jack. Or even to go outside and visit, as she had yesterday. It was a cooler day, more like autumn weather. She didn't even have the excuse of bringing him water.

The day flew by quickly with the steady flow of customers finally thinning out after five. With the store empty, Rachel slipped back to Charlie's playroom. He'd been napping since four and she'd just heard his chirpy wake-up sounds on the baby monitor. Calling her.

"Hello, Charlie. Are you awake?"

She stared down at her baby a moment, a wave of love welling up at the mere sight of him. He lay on his back, playing with his bare feet. His apple cheeks were rosy from his nap and his feathery hair flying in all directions.

"You took off your socks again? Did you have a good nap?" Rachel lifted him up and gave him a hug. "You're raring to go, aren't you?"

Charlie squealed happily, as if answering her.

She changed his diaper and carried him out to the store, where she had a few quick tasks to perform before closing the store.

Jack stood at the counter. He smiled slowly at her, his eyes lighting up at the sight of Charlie.

"The door was open so I let myself in."

"I'm just about to close. I was out back. With Charlie."

"I know. I heard you on the baby monitor," he admitted.

Rachel glanced at him, then looked away. She felt self conscious though she didn't know why.

"How is he doing? Any more teething problems?" Jack glanced at Charlie, looking concerned. He reached out and gently stroked the curve of the baby's cheek with just the tip of his index finger. Charlie gurgled and grabbed the finger.

"He seems much better… How is the roof coming?" she countered, trying to keep the conversation more business-like.

"I put on the first layer of tar paper today. I should start the new shingles by Monday." He paused. "Do you open the shop tomorrow?"

"From noon to four. Sunday is a big day for day-trippers. The other shop keepers on Main Street say that it really gets crowded once the leaves turn."

"Would you like to have dinner with me tomorrow night, after you close? I know it's short notice...but we can take Charlie with us. If you can't find a baby sitter."

There it was. The follow-through on last night's encounter. He was asking on her date...and including Charlie? That had to be a first. Julia had been right. This guy was a rare opportunity.

Rachel had been fretting about this moment all day. But still felt caught off guard. Forgetting all the well-crafted excuses and explanations she'd practiced all day.

Just be honest. Keep it simple. Julia's words of advice echoed in her brain.

She did want to have dinner with him.

So that trashed the honesty plan.

"I appreciate the invitation, Jack...but I don't think that would be a good idea." She tried to sound firm and confident, but knew she wasn't quite pulling it off.

"Really? Why not? It seemed like a very good idea last night."

She hadn't expected him to be so blunt. A lot of things seemed like a good idea last night. She didn't know what to say. "Last night...I think I gave you the wrong idea...unintentionally," she added.

He didn't say anything, looked at her through narrowed eyes and crossed his arms over his chest.

"Are you seeing someone? Is that it?"

"No...not at all...I really don't want to date anyone right now. Especially someone who's doing work for me. I need to focus on Charlie and getting this business off the ground." When he didn't reply, she added, "It's not anything about you, Jack...it's not that I don't like you..."

Wow, was that ever the understatement of her life.

Keep it simple. Don't over explain. Rachel was about to say more, but stopped herself.

"You like me. Well, that's a start." He seemed amused.

And sounded as if he hadn't heard a word of the rest of her little speech.

Rachel didn't know what to say next. Half of her wished he'd just go. The other half wished he'd keep trying to change her mind. She knew it wouldn't take much.

"What if we don't call it a date?" he offered. "What if we call it eating dinner? In the same restaurant. At the same table. I'd just like to spend some time with you, Rachel. Just to talk." When she didn't answer right away, he added, "There's a nice place right in town, The Lion's Head Inn. Or we could eat someplace else if you prefer."

He was charming when he wanted to be, wasn't he? Rachel was finding his invitation hard to resist. It had been a long time since she'd been out for an evening, dining at a nice restaurant. Even with Charlie, it would be a treat.

Did he have to look at her that way? She could feel her resolve melting under the warmth of his dark eyes.

The Lion's Head Inn was a historic inn on the village green and the most expensive place in town. He couldn't afford dinner there. Not on the salary she was paying. It was a gallant gesture.

"No…I'm sorry. I can't," she said simply. From her downcast tone she was sure he could tell how much she wanted to though. Which was practically…embarrassing.

He watched her a moment, waiting for her to say something more. Then he shrugged. "All right. If you say so…I understand," he added.

She wondered if he really did. She'd sent him a message that wasn't entirely true. After only two days in Jack's company, she had to admit that maybe this was one man she could allow into her carefully constructed, well-defended world.

Too late now. You blew it. He's hurt. Rejected. He won't ask again.

That's what I want, right?

Rachel sighed. When he was standing right in front of her, so close she could reach out and touch him, she didn't know what she wanted.

"See you Monday."

"Sure. See you." Rachel nodded, balancing Charlie on her hip.

Jack turned and walked towards the door. She found herself following him a few steps, then stopped.

"Bye, Jack."

He waved at her without turning around, then walked out the door.

What had she done?

Maybe Julia was right. Maybe she was making a stupendous mistake here, throwing back the catch of a lifetime. Okay, he was a happy wanderer type, flashing all signs of commitment phobia.

So? Nobody was perfect.

The man had cleaned up the kitchen without being asked, for goodness sakes.

Rachel sighed. She couldn't stand here and worry about Jack Sawyer anymore. She had to give Charlie his dinner and bath and put him to bed, then work on her sewing. She had some orders to fill and wanted the reputation of prompt turnaround.

She'd told Jack the truth. Mostly. She did need to focus on her son and her business. In that order. Sales this week had not been good. She hadn't reached her goal or even the break even mark. She was starting to get worried. She needed this business to be a success. She needed it for her own peace of mind and in order to stay close to Charlie.

She didn't need any distractions right now and he was turning into a major one.

She twisted the lock on the shop door and flipped the sign to Closed.

It might as well have been a sign on her heart.

Jack stomped out to the old red truck. Turned the key in the ignition with more force than was necessary, then threw the transmission into Reverse, pulled out of the driveway and barreled down Main Street.

When he'd first bought the truck at a used auto lot on the highway, he thought it was great fun, driving around in the heap. Part of his clever disguise.

Tonight, he despised the pathetic, rattling vehicle.

He hated his false identity and self-assigned mission. He hated lying to Rachel Reilly.

If he'd met Rachel as his real self—successful, accomplished, wealthy—she would agree to date him in a heartbeat. He had no doubt. Never mind her "I don't want to get involved with anyone right now. It's not you" speech.

It was him. Or rather the identity he'd assumed. The him she thought he was, Jack's weary brain twirled in a triple-Axel.

He had wondered what she would say if the other Jack Sawyer asked her out.

He had the distinct feeling she hadn't been kissed in a while. For some reason, that thought had cheered him.

It has also sobered him. Stopped him cold in his tracks.

He'd been swept up in something last night. Some irresistible force he'd never quite encountered before. The evening had started off innocently enough and their table talk had yielded some valuable information about her.

But little by little, he'd lost control. Of the situation and his own actions. He could still smell the flowery scent of her skin and hair. It had gone straight to his brain, like a drug.

Back in his room at the Lion's Head Inn, he'd come to his senses. He couldn't let this go any further. He had to tell her the truth. Who he really was, why he'd come up here

He'd come for Charlie but had found something else altogether. He had to get control of the situation. He had to give up this charade.

His plan was to take her out, wine her, dine her, get her to relax and slip into a good frame of mind. Then he'd ease into the truth slowly, so she wouldn't be shocked.

Well, she'd be shocked no matter how he did it.

If they were out in public, he thought he'd have a better chance of her hearing him out. Acting reasonably. Letting him tell his side of the situation.

She'd be angry at the way he'd tricked her. But she'd understand after she cooled down. Wouldn't she?

He hadn't expected her to brush him off. To refuse to spend an evening with him.

Maybe he should have been pleased that she was more particular than she seemed last night. But he wasn't. He'd never expected to feel so…disappointed.

He thought he was asking her out to tell her the truth about their relationship. But now he realized that wasn't all he wanted.

He wanted to see her again, alone. Up close and personal, not just a distant view from the top of a ladder.

He wanted to make her laugh. To see the way her blue eyes changed color ever so slightly as emotions danced over her lovely face. He wanted to hold her in his arms again and kiss her. Again. This time, even longer.

When she was standing right in front of him, so close he could smell her perfume and practically feel the heat of her skin, he didn't know what he wanted.

His BlackBerry sounded, signaling an incoming e-mail. Jack reluctantly flipped it open and read the text message.

More bad news. A crisis on a building project back in New York. If they were sending urgent text messages on a Saturday it had to be bad.

He sighed and hit the Auto dial to return the call.

He checked the time. Nearly six o'clock. He could reach New York by nine. It was going to be a long night.

Chapter Five

"Any word from Jack?" Julia tied an apron around her slim waist and reached for an oven mitt.

Rachel loved sitting in Julia's kitchen. It was state-of-the-art beautiful, with rich granite counter tops, an island work station and warm cherrywood cabinets with all the right touches. And cozy at the same time.

Julia had bought an old farmhouse just outside of town years ago in an estate auction. She'd gotten a bargain basement price for the house and property, which included a barn, woods and a pond. But the purchase had taken real courage... and faith.

The place had been a rundown mess. She'd once shown Rachel pictures. It had looked absolutely haunted.

Little by little, Julia had renovated. The house was turning into a showplace. A real Vermont charmer.

Julia wasn't a great cook, but loved to try new recipes picked up from cooking shows. She often invited Rachel and Charlie over. On Wednesday night, Julia had urged her to come, insisting she needed some moral support, entertaining her mother and her mother's latest beau. But Rachel knew her pal was just trying to cheer her up.

"As a matter of fact, he called just before I left the shop. He says now he won't be back until Thursday."

"First he's coming back Tuesday. Then Wednesday...now *Thursday?* Did he tell you anything else about this mysterious emergency?"

Rachel shook her head. "He just keeps saying the same thing. It's another project and he's sorry. It can't be helped. He hopes I'll be patient.... He's disappearing on me, isn't he?"

"Not necessarily. You do have a contract."

Rachel wasn't just worried about the work getting done. Not entirely. They both knew that. But it was nice of Julia to pretend that was the main concern.

"Have you paid him much yet?"

"I haven't paid him anything."

"Really? That's funny. Most contractors ask for at least a small part up front. To buy supplies and keep their end running."

"He didn't ask so I didn't think of it. Is that bad?"

"It's good for you, if he is going to fade into the horizon. But since no money has exchanged hands, it does make the contract less binding."

"Let's face it, Jules. If the guy wants to back out of the agreement, I'm not going to hunt him down. I don't have the time or the resources."

"Right. And he knows that too."

"So...you think he's fading into the sunset?"

Julia shrugged. She poured some wine into Rachel's glass and then her own. "It's hard to say. Maybe he has some family situation somewhere that he doesn't want to talk about. Or a business problem. It could be anything."

"Maybe he's a fugitive from the law. Or has a wife and kids stashed away somewhere." Rachel's tone was joking, though the suspicion had crossed her mind.

Julia met Rachel's glance and looked away. "I'm sorry I encouraged you to get involved with him. You were right. He is a bit...flaky. Even if he did the dishes."

"You were only trying to help," Rachel told her friend.

Julia glanced at her, then reached in the oven and pulled out a tray of spinach and cheese puffs, wrapped in pastry. She slipped them onto a plate and set it out on the counter where they sat.

Rachel inhaled the buttery aroma. "Gee, those smell good. Did you make them yourself?"

Julia nodded. "Try one. The spinach part is healthy."

Right. The rest of the ingredients were a diet disaster.

Julia served Rachel a pastry and then served herself. "So, he's coming back Thursday?"

"So he says. I'll believe it when I see it." Rachel cut a bite with her fork and took a tiny taste. It was perfectly yummy.

She gave herself the green light to eat the whole portion.

What did it matter? Jack had disappeared. She didn't have any pressing reason to lose her baby weight now.

Thursday morning, Rachel woke to the sound of a hammer, pounding nails in the cottage roof. She grabbed the alarm clock and checked the time with sleep bleary eyes. Exactly seven. She was lucky her neighbors weren't the complaining type.

Jack had returned and started early. To make up for lost time. He'd not only lost time on this job, he'd lost her trust. And good opinion.

As she jumped out of bed and pulled on her robe, she suddenly realized she was angry at him. Steaming, blazing angry for walking out on the work he'd promised to do, without any explanation.

Angry for leading her on, getting her hopes up. The way he'd been so attentive to her and Charlie...and then just dropped off the face of the earth.

Add "emotional tease," "totally unreliable" and "no follow through" to the list of reasons I should never get involved with him.

Dressed for the day, with Charlie balanced on her hip, she glanced briefly out the window at him. The most annoying thing of all was, it had been so long since she'd met a man that made her feel this way. She still felt attracted to him, despite his bad behavior. She just wanted to shut it off. Where in the world was her Reset button?

Rachel's anger felt like a low-frequency hum in the back of her brain. She silently fumed all morning, as she waited on customers or handled her varied phone calls. The tap-tap-tap of Jack's hammer in the background, a persistent reminder that the object of her ire was out there.

She waited all morning for him to come to the shop and make some excuse for his lapse. She saw his truck leave in the middle of the day. A half hour later, she saw him return. Instead of heading to the cottage, he headed toward the shop door. Rachel readied herself, though she wasn't sure what would happen.

"Hello, Rachel," he said evenly. "I'm back."

"So I noticed."

"I want to apologize again for the interruption in the project. I'm sure I can make up the time. Something came up," he added. "An emergency."

"Yes, you told me that." Rachel's voice was curt. She was holding heavy books of sample announcement cards and baptism invitations. She let them drop on the counter with a thump.

"We have a contract," she reminded him.

He looked as if he wanted to smile, but was forcing himself not to. "Yes, I'm aware of that."

"You didn't seem be aware for the past five days. I thought you understood that I need that cottage in rentable condition by the end of the month. I'm depending on it."

He nodded, all traces of humor gone from his rugged features. "I do understand. I'll have it done as fast as I possibly can. If it's not completed by your deadline, I'll make up the difference in your income myself. How's that?"

"Pretty good...if I could only believe it."

She could tell that her words had stung him, but he didn't counter. "Be honest, Jack. Were you...mad at me or something? Is that why you took off?"

"Mad at you? Why would I be?" He looked genuinely puzzled, then a lightbulb went on. "Because you didn't want to go out with me?" He almost laughed and Rachel felt embarrassed she'd been so straightforward. "Don't worry, Rachel. I wasn't crushed by your rejection."

"I didn't say crushed. Maybe resentful is a better term for it."

He sighed, looking suddenly serious. "I apologize again for the disappearing act. But I did have an emergency. If I could tell you anything more, I would. My absence had nothing to do with you. I don't know if there's anything else I can say."

Rachel stared at him.

"Fine. I feel the same."

He met her gaze and she couldn't look away. "I wish you weren't so mad at me, Rachel."

"Don't worry, I'll get over it." She hadn't intended to sound harsh...and hurt, her tone implying she'd get over a lot of things. Any romantic notions she had about him, for instance.

She couldn't keep the angry edge from her voice. She was disappointed. She couldn't help it. Or hide it very well either.

He said goodbye and left the shop.

Rachel felt very sad and empty. She hoped he would stick to his word this time and finish as quickly as possible.

The sooner she saw Jack Sawyer go for good, the better.

"What a cute costume. Is that one for sale somewhere?"

The woman had been browsing around Rachel's booth at

the fall fair for quite a while. Now she stared down at Charlie who was wearing one of Rachel's original designs, a purple dinosaur with pale green wings and a long swishy tail.

"That's a sample. I mostly make them to order." The woman looked disappointed that she couldn't walk away with the purchase. "It can be finished in a week and you choose any colors you like," Rachel encouraged her. "Here are the fabrics…"

She showed the woman a chart with squares of material. The idea of having some say in the design held her interest.

A short time later, Rachel was writing up an order for two costumes, one pink and lavender, the other black and orange.

The Blue Lake Fall Fair ran for two days, the last weekend in September. There had been a larger crowd on Saturday but the real shoppers had come out today, Rachel noticed.

The booth had been an investment she probably couldn't afford, but she was partly here for advertising, not just to sell her merchandise. Sometimes she wondered if having her shop at the very end of Main Street was going to be her undoing. Even when tourists made it all the way to her store, they were often "shopped out" and didn't want to spend any more.

She felt the familiar financial pressures flocking around her head and tried to brush them aside. She had taken a lot of orders today, on the costumes, quilts and even her toys. Julia's mother, Lucy, had stopped by to help her in the afternoon and had also watched Charlie awhile. Lucy was great with the customers. She could start a conversation with anybody.

It was still a long haul to sit here, manning this booth basically on her own for two days. She hoped the effort would be worth it. The weekend had certainly brought home to her the fact that she was indeed an independent operator. Having it all, but having it all alone, with all the work and pressures that came along with her freedom.

As if a sign from the universe, reminding her that she still had a few friends, Julia appeared.

"Sorry I took so long to come by. The office has been crazy today. A lot of lookers, but maybe I'll get a lead or two."

Julia stepped into the booth and plunked down in an empty chair. She caught sight of Charlie in his costume and sighed with delight. "Look at this cute little dinosaur! Is he for sale?"

"Not quite. You can hold him though if you like." Charlie held out his arms to Julia and she scooped him up. "I'd be delighted…if he doesn't bite. Are you going to bite me, Mr. Dinosaur?" she teased him.

"Watch out, he hasn't eaten for a while," Rachel warned.

"How's it going? Selling much today?"

"There were more people here yesterday but more real shoppers today."

Julia shrugged. "Serious fall-fair-goers. They're already starting their Christmas shopping." Julia touched Charlie's hand and began to play a clapping game. "So, how's it going with Jack?"

Rachel had a feeling she was building up to that.

"We haven't spoken in two days. Just as well," she added. "I've been really busy getting everything ready for the booth. I hardly noticed."

Julia rolled her eyes. "Right."

"I hear him working out there. He finished the roof and started inside." While she was glad of the progress, now she got to see him even less since he was hidden from her sight. "I just want him to finish and go."

Julia glanced at her, playing a clap-clap game with Charlie. "At least the roof is done. It looks like it might rain. You won't have to worry."

The day had started off sunny and windless, with just the right touch of fall in the air to bring out a fairgoing crowd. But sometime after lunch, nickel-colored clouds had gathered and a chilly breeze blew leaves from the treetops that surrounded the village green.

Rachel had brought extra clothes and blankets for Charlie. But was still concerned keeping him outdoors all day.

"It is getting colder. I might leave early."

"Good idea." Julia glanced at her watch. "Want some help? I need to take over for someone at an open house. But I have a few minutes."

"That's okay." Rachel noticed a fresh bunch of shoppers heading down her lane, a chatty group of women who were each carrying two and three shopping bags. "I can stick it out a while longer."

Julia gently placed Charlie back in his stroller. "Back in you go, Dinosaur. See you later." She stood up and buttoned her leather jacket. "Don't get stuck out here in the rain, okay? I'll feel terrible."

Rachel laughed at her reasoning. "Okay. I don't want you to feel bad. I won't get stuck."

Her friend smiled and set off for the parking lot.

As Rachel had hoped, the group of eager shoppers descended and kept her busy for a long time. When they finally left, she had made almost as many sales in one hour as she had all afternoon.

As she looked over the orders, a fat cold raindrop struck the page. Then another. And another.

She quickly pulled up the cover on Charlie's stroller, so that he was completely protected. Then she ran around, trying to gather her merchandise as half of blew away in the wind.

A heavy gust filled the sides of her cloth booth like sails on a ship. She heard the merchants around her cry out, as one or two of the booths blew over.

She stuffed her baby sweaters, hats and blankets into the nylon duffel bags as fast as she could. But she felt as if she was moving in slow motion. The rain pelted down, making it hard to see what she was doing.

Charlie started crying. He was scared. She abandoned her table of merchandise and ran to him.

A strong hand rested a hand on her shoulder, as she bent over the stroller. "Get him inside. I'll take care of this."

She recognized the voice with a jolt.

It was Jack.

She turned to face him. The rain had flattened his dark hair and ran down his hard features.

"Meet me at the inn. Wait in the lobby." Jack pointed to the Lion's Head Inn, straight across the green.

People were dispersing in every direction. It seemed as good a place as any to meet up with him.

"Okay...thanks," she shouted at him over the wind. She grabbed the stroller handles and pushed it across the green, just about running, and glanced back at Jack.

He'd pulled one of the fabric walls of the booth up and across, creating a shelter from the rain over his head. He already had most of the table cleared and the clothes that hung on display packed away.

She looked back at where she was going and quickly reached the inn. The porch had a handicapped ramp and she steered the stroller up and under the porch roof.

A crowd of drenched fairgoers huddled there, staring out at the rain. A few moved aside to make room when they realized she had a baby.

She'd barely gotten a breath and unzipped Charlie's cover. The baby looked stunned, but basically fine. And quite dry, Rachel noticed.

She heard a thump and her duffel bags of merchandise appeared at her feet. Then she looked up and saw Jack, looking winded but triumphant. And soaked to the skin.

Rain poured off every inch of him, his clothes were soaked through, his thick hair slicked back. Rain dripped off his chin, his nose and even his ear lobes.

She hadn't been this close to him in days and he'd never

looked better. She felt an almost irresistible urge to lick all the rain drops off his skin.

"Wow, that came out nowhere." He shook his head, like a dog who just had a bath.

"So did you," she pointed out, still stunned by his super hero performance.

He laughed. "Is that any way to thank me? I just saved you and Charlie…and half the inventory from your store… from drowning."

Rachel felt adequately shamed. "Thank you, Jack. Thanks for your help."

Again, she wanted to add.

"I was at the fair. Just…checking it out."

Had he come to look for her? After their long days of cold shoulders? The notion was comforting and disturbing at the same time.

He crouched down and peered into Charlie's stroller. "Is he okay? He didn't get wet, did he?"

"All the commotion scared him. But otherwise he's just fine. I guess I pulled the cover up right away. I think he's perfectly dry."

Jack glanced at her, he seemed to be fighting a smile. "That little boy gets excellent care. I know that already."

He slung the strap of one bag over his shoulder and picked up the other with his hand. Then he rested his free hand on her shoulder. "Let's get inside. I need to change out of these wet clothes. Are you hungry? I think the dining room is open. We might as well have dinner while we wait for the rain to stop."

Rachel felt herself led along to the entrance to the lobby. Dinner sounded good. She was tired and starving.

But with Jack? And he was going to change into dry clothes? Had she heard him right?

He quickly picked up on her puzzled expression.

"I'm staying here while I'm working at your place. I'm sort of between apartments. And it seemed convenient."

She knew she shouldn't stare at him, but she couldn't help it. He didn't have much sense about money, did he? She wasn't cheating him for his work, but she certainly wasn't paying top dollar. She knew his profits had to be slim and here he was, blowing it all on a stay at this inn.

"Isn't it…expensive to stay here that long?"

"I got a discount. Because I took the room for a long stay." When she seemed unconvinced he added, "I write it off my taxes. It all works out in the end to my advantage."

She sighed. Well, what did it matter to her how he spent the money he was earning?

He led her into the lobby, decorated in flawless Victorian period style with antique settees, potted plants and fan backed upholstered arm chairs. "Wait right here. I won't be very long."

Rachel didn't reply. She wasn't sure if she was going to stay. That didn't seem very wise, all things considered.

"I'll bring you down a dry shirt or something," he added as he walked away.

There, that was another reason. How was she going to keep any emotional distance at all, wearing his clothes?

Charlie made a fretful sound. She unstrapped him and took him out of the stroller. She knew he must be hungry by now and took out a bottle for him from his baby bag.

There were one or two dry cotton blankets in his stroller and she set one across her lap, so he wouldn't get wet from her damp pants. He drank eagerly and relaxed in her arms, his eyelids growing heavy and drooping down at half mast.

She felt the same. Perhaps it was the rush of excitement during the storm or the entire day of working outdoors. She felt so drained she didn't have the energy—or will—to sneak away from Jack.

And she didn't have the heart to disturb Charlie while he contentedly downed his formula. He'd been such a trouper all day. As she gazed down at Charlie, she felt she didn't deserve such a beautiful, wonderful little boy.

She didn't care if her entire store blew away. He was all she needed in the entire world.

Jack returned just as Rachel was patting Charlie's back for a burp. She hadn't seen for days and now drank in the sight of him. Fresh from a shower, his thick dark hair was combed back wet, emphasizing the strong lines of his face and large dark eyes. His cheeks were freshly shaven, looking so smooth she was tempted to test them. He wore an ocean blue sweater with a rolled collar, the sleeves pushed up to emphasize his muscular arms and broad shoulder. A tantalizing hint of chest hair showed at the opening of the collar.

All in all, he looked impossibly handsome, like an advertisement for male sex appeal.

Especially when he stood over her, smiling down with an expression she couldn't quite fathom.

"Here's something dry for you to wear. You'll disappear in it. But you'll be a lot more comfortable."

Rachel took the sweater he offered. Soft, black…cashmere? This man had good taste, you had to hand him that.

"Here, let me take Charlie. You can go change and we'll go into dinner."

"Okay. I'll be right back." Rachel didn't feel up to an argument. Or ready to go back into the downpour.

She handed over Charlie carefully. The baby often didn't like to go to strangers and got nervous and cried. But he went to Jack willingly and settled in his arms.

Jack looked proud, holding him in the crook of one arm.

"Just hang out with me a minute, pal. Mom will be right back."

Rachel ran off to the Ladies' Room, wondering why the sight of Jack holding Charlie had caused a little lump in her throat.

In the Ladies' Room, she peeled off her wet jacket and then her wet cotton jersey underneath. Her bra was dry. Thank goodness. She didn't need a wet bra clinging to the sweater.

She pulled on the sweater, which felt like velvet against

her skin. The rain and wind had chilled her but the soft cashmere was cozy and warming. An excellent choice, she thought, giving Jack credit.

Yet, when she checked the mirror, she found a major problem.

The sweater had V-neck and was also quite big on her. Hence, the neckline drooped to dangerous proportions.

Contrary to Jack's prediction, she had *not* disappeared in the garment. If anything, she was even more visible. Especially certain parts.

She considered putting on the wet shirt again. But just couldn't bring herself to do it. She tugged on the shoulders, and neckline, getting it into decent territory. Finally it was right. She'd have to keep her eye on this all night.

She didn't want to give Jack the wrong idea.

Don't worry, the rest of you will definitely scare him off. He won't want to come anywhere near you, a little voice posed.

She did look a wreck. She nearly gasped out loud finally facing a mirror.

Her hair appeared to be glued to her head and the small amount of eye makeup she'd started off with that morning had melted into dark rings under her eyes.

He wanted to have dinner with…this?

Wow, he really must like me.

She tugged the band out of her scraggly pony tail and spread her hair with her fingers. It looked just as bad…there was just more of it now.

Then she spotted the hand dryer on the wall and decided to give it a try.

With her head tipped over, she smacked the drier to turn it on. She stayed that way until the blood rushed to her head and she felt sort of dizzy. When she stood up, her curly hair had dried out and fluffed up almost perfectly.

She felt a little dizzy from the process, but the improvement was encouraging. Digging through her purse like a golden retriever searching for a buried bone, she finally came up with a tube of concealer and a pink lip gloss. She did what she could with her limited resources. Then stepped back.

Well, considering how I looked walking in, it wasn't bad for a rest room makeover.

Maybe she could pitch the idea as a new reality show.

She stepped out to the lobby again and spotted Jack with Charlie. His back was turned to her as he held Charlie up to a painting of animals, a reproduction of "Peaceable Kingdom."

She heard Jack patiently pointing out each animal, telling Charlie its name. The baby was very attentive, staring wide eyed and mimicking Jack's pointing gestures, though she knew he couldn't understand a word.

Jack turned, as if he'd sensed her approach. His eyes lit up, clearly pleased at her transformation.

She suddenly realized he'd gotten his way tonight. He wanted to take her to dinner at this inn, Charlie included. And here they were.

For the life of her, Rachel couldn't remember why she'd put up such a fight about it.

Dinner went well. Better than Rachel expected. Even Charlie seemed to be having a good time.

It was hard to stay angry at Jack when he'd saved her from the rain storm and hard to be angry at anyone in the elegant restaurant he'd chosen.

"Would your son like another banana, sir?" The waiter asked Jack in a serious tone.

Jack glanced at Rachel. "I'm not sure. Better check with his mother."

Rachel thought it odd that he hadn't corrected the waiter's mistake, but she thought maybe Jack hadn't heard him. Or didn't think the assumption was such a big deal.

Charlie had eaten a decent meal for a baby dining out. Some beef, mashed potatoes and broccoli. Then the banana, just to keep him busy.

"I think he's okay for now."

"How about some ice cream? Can Charlie eat ice cream yet?"

"Well...sure. I'm not sure if he's ever had it. Someone has to help him with it," she warned.

"I'll feed it to him," Jack offered. "Bring him a little bowl of ice cream. Some vanilla, I guess." He glanced at Rachel and she approved with a smile.

Jack looked so excited. You'd think it was the first time he was going to eat ice cream.

"Would you like some dessert?" Jack asked. "They have a nice list."

Rachel shook her head. "The duck was wonderful. I couldn't eat another bite."

They both ordered coffee and the waiter departed. A silence fell over the table. She looked over at Jack.

"Dinner was wonderful, Jack. It really was a treat for me. Thanks for taking me here...and Charlie."

"My pleasure. I thought you'd enjoy it."

"You were right," she said graciously.

He smiled very slowly at her. "I'm glad you're not mad anymore."

She shook head. "You made up for it."

He looked down and fiddled with a teaspoon. "I understand why you were angry. I want to tell you where I went last week. Give you a real explanation—"

Rachel cut him off. "You don't have to. I was wrong for prying. You don't owe me any explanations."

"But I want to tell you, Rachel. It's...important."

As much as she wanted to know the full truth, she also believed it was important tonight to keep the lines clearly drawn. Yes, she could enjoy a well deserved night out in his company. But this wasn't going to lead to anything more.

She didn't want to share the intimate details of his life. She didn't want to get any closer to him. To build up false hopes and illusions. That's what these kinds of conversations led to.

Being perfectly honest with herself, she knew that some part of her was also afraid to hear the truth. Sure, her theories with Julia had been outlandish. But if Jack really did have a family stashed somewhere...or had a date with a parole officer...she really didn't want to know.

"It's fine. Honestly," she insisted. "It's your own business. If it doesn't have to do with the work on the cottage, I really don't want to know about it," she insisted.

Jack looked confounded, but as if he was gearing up to try another tack with her.

Charlie's ice cream arrived, two large scoops in a frosty silver dish. The waiter didn't think to give it to Jack but placed it down right in front of the baby, who sat in a booster seat between them.

Charlie went at it with both hands, then stuffed his ice cream coated fingers in his mouth. Jack jumped up but couldn't catch him in time.

Charlie's gurgles and contented expression made them both laugh out loud.

"He's got fast hands. Great for football," Jack nodded at Rachel eagerly. Using the spoon he gently tried to wipe some of the ice cream off Charlie's face and body.

"Oh, I don't want him to play football. That's too rough. Kids get hurt."

"What do mean? He's got to play football. I played football," he offered. "I never got hurt."

She wasn't sure what that had to with anything. By the time Charlie started asking her if he could indulge in the barbaric sport, Jack would be far gone from their lives.

"Look at those shoulders. He's got the perfect build. He's fast, too. I've seen him crawl."

"Jack...he's only ten months old. I don't think I should worry about it yet."

She gave him a look that put him at a distance.

"Sure. It's your call. Entirely. Just a suggestion," he said lightly.

The waiter stopped by. "Anything else, sir?"

"Just the check, please," Jack flipped open his wallet and took out a credit card.

The parable of the grasshopper and the ant came to mind.

She sighed. Jack was definitely a grasshopper. Too bad for her.

As they left the restaurant, Jack's mood seemed subdued. Rachel had cleaned Charlie up at the table with a wipe, and Jack held both his hands, helping him walk to the lobby.

This was the back-breaking stage that Rachel found wearing. She was glad to see Jack give it a try.

"He can almost walk," Jack remarked. "He practically has his balance. Isn't ten months young?"

"Some kids start sooner. I know it sounds selfish, but I'm not really looking forward to him being mobile," she confessed. "I'm afraid I won't be able to keep up with him."

Jack glanced at her. "You might be right... Maybe you need some help."

"Like a sitter, you mean?"

"No...like a husband," he said bluntly. He glanced up at her, then back down at Charlie again.

There were out in the lobby and Jack picked Charlie up in his arms. Rachel didn't know how to answer, so she didn't say anything.

"I can drive you back in my truck and get your car tomorrow," he offered.

Ever helpful. Was he auditioning for the job?

Stop it, Rachel. Do not let your mind go down that path. Emotional tease, remember?

"I'd better take my own car. It has Charlie's car seat," she reminded him.

"Oh, right. Is it far?"

"Just near the green."

"I'll walk you out. I can bring your duffel bags tomorrow."

The duffel bags. She'd been having such a nice time, she'd forgotten all about the fair and even the rainstorm that had brought them together.

They stepped out on to the porch of the old inn. The sky was clear and cloudless, the air considerably cooler. Stars dotted a velvet blue sky and a crescent moon glowed with an orange hue.

"Rain stopped," Jack observed. "I guess we'll get to see what kind of job I did on your new roof…I haven't done one of those in a while. Hope I didn't forget any steps."

She could tell he was teasing and she just shook her head at him. "Right, we'll see. I'll check tomorrow."

They stepped out on the green. Jack pushed the stroller along the path while Rachel held Charlie in her arms. He seemed suddenly sleepy and she knew she'd have no trouble putting him to bed tonight.

"Stop by. I enjoy our visits. They break up the day," he added with a sly grin.

They'd reached her SUV. Rachel clicked open the locks and fitted Charlie in his car seat. Jack folded up the stroller and stowed in the trunk.

"Did you ever get that tire fixed?"

"Um…no. Guess I forgot about it," she admitted.

"You shouldn't drive around without it. I'll take it in for you tomorrow."

He couldn't help himself, could he? She didn't even argue with him.

"Okay…thanks. And thanks again for dinner. It was lovely…I'm glad we're friends again, Jack," she added.

She was sitting in the car with the window rolled down.

Jack stood outside, one hand on the edge of the door frame.
He looked surprised by the term. "Is that what we are?"

"Yes, of course." She willed her voice to sound firm,

though inside she felt suddenly shaky. The way he was looking at her, his face close enough to lean inside and kiss her again.

She could tell he was thinking the same thing.

He began to lean forward, to do just that. She almost couldn't resist. Then suddenly she pulled back to a safe distance.

"Jack...please. Let's just keep it...uncomplicated. You'll be leaving here in a week or two. It doesn't make any sense to me in getting involved."

"Right." He nodded and stepped back. "Even if you were interested in a relationship right now...which you're not. I remember," he said curtly.

She could tell he was hurt again. Or mad. Or both.

But was that her fault?

Was he going to pull his disappearing act again?

"I get it. Case closed, Rachel."

She sighed. She didn't like hearing him say that, either.

There was no good outcome here, she decided. She started the engine of her SUV and waved to him.

"See you tomorrow, Jack." *I hope*, she added under her breath.

He stepped back as she pulled away—but didn't answer.

Chapter Six

Rachel woke early and found the cupboard bare. She'd been so busy with the fair the last few days, she didn't even have milk in the house. She dressed herself and Charlie quickly, gave the baby a bottle of juice, then bundled him into the jogging stroller and headed up Main Street to the Blue Lake Delicatessen.

Sunday's downpour had washed away the last traces of summer. The morning air was crisp, the sunlight bright, shining down through trees that had already lost some foliage in the storm. The colored leaves were scattered on the sidewalk, like party confetti the morning after. She loved the palate of it all, the way the unlikely colors blended perfectly—golds, oranges, burgundies.

She picked up a few particularly spectacular specimens along the way and handed them down to Charlie to play with.

It seemed autumn had officially arrived, overnight, while they were sleeping.

The tiny store was filled. A long line of customers waited

at the deli counter for take-away breakfast and lunches. Working men mostly, on their way to a job. Rachel thought she wouldn't have been surprised to find Jack in the lineup. There were also some people in jogging suits. The deli was a crossroads for all types who lived in the village.

It was also a physics mystery, how so much varied merchandise could be packed into so small a space. The store never failed to amaze Rachel, offering everything from eggs to fishing tackle, beer nuts to buttons, dog food to dead bolts.

If you couldn't find what you were looking for, the owners, Lou and Ella Krueger, would disappear into a back room and usually emerge with your heart's desire.

Feeling invigorated from her walk, Rachel strolled the narrow store aisles and quickly gathered up some staples— milk, eggs, bread and peanut butter. She brought it all to the register where Mrs. Krueger greeted her with a smile. "Hey, Rachel. How's that little boy today? Is he walking yet?"

"Not quite yet. He's working on it."

"Pretty soon you can send him up here to do your shopping."

"Oh, I think we have a while to wait on that."

"Can I give him a cookie?"

"He hasn't had breakfast yet."

"Its oatmeal," Mrs. Krueger made an innocent face. "I can see this is your first. Let's see if you can keep that 'no cookies before breakfast rule' after three or four."

Three…or four? Rachel thought Charlie would be her only, but she didn't bother to argue with Ella Krueger about it. She took the cookie the older woman offered and handed it down to Charlie's eager little hands. It was oatmeal, she reminded herself.

A bushel of shiny red apples near the register caught Rachel's eye. "Those look yummy. What kind are they?"

Rachel had grown up thinking there were only two kinds of apples, red and yellow. And sometimes green, but green were so bitter tasting they didn't seem to count. Since arriving in Vermont she'd been fully indoctrinated about apples, learning about the hundreds of varieties, the melodious names. Fuji and Macoun. Empire, Courtland and Pink Lady.

"Those are Macoun. Just picked yesterday."

"I guess it's really fall," Rachel took a small paper bag and picked out a few apples.

"I'll say it is. The Leaf Peepers should be hitting town any minute. You'd better prepare yourself."

Rachel smiled, thinking the old woman sounded as if she was warning everyone about the end of the world.

"Is it that bad?"

"Bad?" Mrs. Krueger shook her head and chuckled. "It's all good, dear. All good. They spend hours in here, they think it's all so quaint and…retro. Is that the word?"

Rachel nodded. "I think so."

"Lou and I set out some homey-looking displays, syrup bottles and cheddar cheese. We make a killing, then we go to Florida in February. Daytona Beach. Ever been?"

Rachel shook her head. "No, not that area."

"Well, prepare yourself. That's all I can tell you."

Rachel paid and gathered up her bag of groceries, which she stashed in the bottom of the stroller. "Okay, I'll try. Thanks for the warning."

Rachel had heard other shopkeepers in town talk about the flood of tourists that would arrive during the early fall. No one so far had been as explicit as Ella Krueger, though.

If her predictions were true, Rachel thought her financial crunch might soon be solved. But maple syrup, cheddar cheese and antiques were one thing. Baby clothes were another.

As if to answer her doubts, she heard a roar approaching down the quiet street. She turned to see not one, but two long silver touring buses roll down Main Street, headed for the village green.

She smiled down at Charlie. "Let the games begin."

* * *

Rachel ran into her shop and did exactly as Mrs. Krueger suggested. She prepared. She ran about, putting the merchandise in order and making sure the clothes, quilts and toys were all attractively displayed.

Then she ran outside and checked the window.

Not bad, considering she'd been totally distracted when she made the display. She thought she could add a few more autumnal touches.

Jack's truck pulled up the drive and she turned to greet him. He parked near the house, instead driving up the cottage. Then he took out the duffel bags of merchandise he'd rescued at the fair and brought to them her.

He wore a black thermal vest over a long sleeved gray jersey, along with his usual worn jeans and work boots. The vest made him look a bit like a member of a S.W.A.T. team. He could apprehend her any time. She wouldn't mind it.

"Oh, thanks for bringing that back. I forgot all about it."

"No problem. I'll bring it into the shop."

Rachel followed him up the walk to the door, then reached around him and opened it. She was suddenly very close to him, so close her lips could have grazed his freshly shaven cheek. He smelled good, like soap and aftershave. And some other scent distinctly his own.

She could tell by the way his body stiffened, he sensed it too.

She stepped back and the door swung open.

"Thanks," he said curtly. "Where do you want this stuff?"

"Let's see…stick them behind the counter for now. I have to sort through everything in there later. Listen, did you happen to find a sign with the shop's name and logo on it?"

Rachel had made a large, hand painted sign for her booth that she thought would be perfect now to stick out in the road, to attract more customers to the store.

"Sorry, I didn't see that. I can go back and look. The town maintenance crews are just cleaning up the square."

"That's okay. I can make another one."

He smiled down at her with a quizzical look. "You seem sort of excited today, Rachel. Anything going on?"

"The Leaf Peepers. They're here. I saw two full buses pull into town this morning. Mrs. Krueger—at the deli?—she says they'll buy anything. She and her husband spend February in Daytona Beach."

He gave her half smile, a tantalizing dimple marking his cheek. "Daytona Beach, huh? If I'm looking for palm trees in February, I prefer St. Bart's or Antigua. I mean, if I could afford a winter vacation," he added.

"I wouldn't know. I've never been to any of those places. The thing is, it's not just Mrs. Krueger. I saw two full buses pull into town this morning."

He nodded. "Yes, I know. They pulled right up to the Inn. I've been bumped out of my room and there isn't a vacancy left in town."

"Oh…that's too bad. There's a motel out on the highway," she said, thinking aloud. "It's a little tacky…" and probably not very clean, she realized, though she didn't add that.

"The desk clerk at the Inn gave me the number. I've already called. They have a vacancy for a few nights, but I can't stay over the weekends.… Not until after Thanksgiving."

"Oh…well, that doesn't work then."

She glanced at him, then back at the store window.

She had a spare room in her apartment. She used it as work space, to sew and fill orders. There was also a futon there, for guests to sleep over. But offering the room to Jack didn't seem a good idea at all.

Rachel knew her willpower would never hold out if they were sleeping under the same roof. She might as well tell him to bring his bags right up to her bedroom.

"What about the cottage? Do you think I could stay there tonight, until I figure it out?"

He was obviously anxious about asking the favor and Rachel was surprised, after all he'd done for her.

"Of course you can. But is it habitable?" she asked him.

"The roof is sealed. The plumbing is working. I can clean out that back bedroom later. I think there's even an old bed frame in there.

"Yes, there is," Rachel answered. "I wrapped the mattress up and put it away so it wouldn't get musty. It's in the basement. I can give you sheets and towels and...things."

It was silly and adolescent, but she felt self-conscious talking about mattresses and bed linens with him. The words conjured up certain unavoidable images. He seemed to sense it, too, she thought and smiled quietly at her.

"Well, whatever you can spare will be fine. I'm sure I can find some acceptable place to stay by tomorrow."

"Yes, I'm sure you can. I'll ask around. Maybe Julia knows of something."

"Good idea." He nodded and pulled out the keys to his truck.

"I'd better get to work. And you need to get ready for the Leaf Peepers," he reminded her with a teasing grin.

"Yes, I do," she answered in a serious tone. "I need to prepare myself."

Jack laughed and shook his head.

Jack clearly thought she was being silly with all her excitement and anticipation about the fall tourist season.

But Rachel was not disappointed. Sales during the morning were brisk and even better in the afternoon. She was busy all day and stayed open until six, a full half hour later than her usual time.

There had been a short break in the afternoon. She took a minute to have a quick snack that served as lunch and bring Jack the sheets, towels and a few other necessary items he needed for the cottage. He'd put the old bed together and claimed everything was fine and he didn't need her help at all to set up the bedroom.

It was just as well, Rachel reflected. All she could imagine was the two of them, rolling around on the mattress. Before the sheets had even been unfolded.

When she finally closed the shop door, she was tired, hungry and eager to count up her receipts for the day.

She'd been so immersed, she hadn't even noticed that Jack had finished work for the day and left. When she went up to her apartment his truck was gone from the driveway.

He must have gone to get some dinner, she realized. She'd considered inviting him to eat with her and Charlie again, but for one thing, she was too tired to cook. For another, she didn't want to set up another situation she couldn't handle.

She fed Charlie and gave him a bath. He had been a bit fussy today. She wondered if it was more teeth coming in. He still seemed a little cranky, unlike his usual, easy temperament. She thought he might be overtired from staying out too late the night before.

"A good night's sleep and you'll feel good as new," she whispered as she rocked him. His soft cheek against her own felt a little warm. But he'd just come out of a warm bath and had on his flannel pajamas. Maybe the one-piece sleep suit was overdoing it a little, Rachel thought. It was cooler out, but not deep winter yet.

He fell asleep quickly. She didn't even need to pace up and down the room and hum "Rockin' Robin." She kissed him again and laid him down in his crib, settling the white stuffed dog beside him.

Rachel went to the window to pull down the shade. She noticed Jack's truck wasn't back yet. She wondered if he had fixed the cottage for himself today. Or maybe made other plans and didn't bother to tell her?

That would be just his style.

And don't you dare forget it.

Rachel showered, checked on Charlie one more time, then got into bed with a thick book. A few pages into the stirring, historical she felt herself falling asleep. She put the book aside and shut the light.

With any luck, there would be another big day at the shop tomorrow.

Then, another...and another.

At least until the end of October, she speculated. Or did Leaf Peepers keep coming up until Thanksgiving?

She made a mental note to check with Ella Krueger.

She wasn't sure what time it was when Charlie's shrill cries woke her. She jumped out of bed and didn't even stop to check the clock. She ran to the baby's room, where he had pulled himself up on the edge of his crib railing. He stood there red-faced and wailing, his damp hair plastered to his little head.

She pulled him out of the crib and held him close. His body was fiery hot.

A fever. A very high one. Hugging him close, she ran to the medicine chest and found the thermometer. The instant ear kind. She set the fussing baby down on the changing table and took his temperature.

One hundred and four?

Her heart jumped to her throat. That couldn't be right.

She did it again, nearly jumping out of her skin at the quick beeping sound.

Same result. One hundred and four.

Charlie was still crying. Her efforts to soothe him had only quieted him down a little. She picked him up and held him close. She felt alarmed. Panicked. She didn't know what to do first.

He'd been sick and run fevers before, but never this high.

She tried to remember what she'd read in her baby books, scanning the book cases in the hallway to find them. Where were the baby books? Ever since she'd moved from New York, all of her books had been in disorder.

He could go into a convulsion...couldn't he?

She took Charlie back in the bathroom and looked for some fever medication. The familiar orange bottle was nowhere to be found. Then she remembered it was down in the kitchen. She had to give him some the day he was teething so badly.

She took Charlie downstairs, set him in his high chair and quickly found the medicine. He still took it in a baby syringe, that squirted the medication down his throat.

Now where had that gone? It wasn't in its usual place, in a plastic bag near the bottle.

Finally, she found it, at the back of the cabinet. She clutched it like a prize.

A knock sounded on the back door. Rachel nearly jumped out of skin and the sound made Charlie cry even louder. She saw Jack peering through the glass and ran over to answer it.

"I heard Charlie crying and saw all the lights on. Is anything the matter?"

So he had come back. She'd never seen the truck return.

She felt a wave of utter relief at the sight of him…and a wave of something else she didn't want to think about too closely just then.

He'd obviously jumped right of bed and didn't have much on. A pair of blue jeans. Nothing else.

She'd seen him bare chested before, but up close and personal, it was a different ball game.

"Charlie's sick. He has a fever. It's very high. I'm trying to give him some medicine…." Rachel explained as she ran back to the baby, who was cying and rubbing the side of his head with his hand.

"How can I help? Just tell me what to do." Jack's expression was serious but controlled.

"I'm just trying to give him this medicine. It will bring the fever down. It's easier if someone holds him."

"Here, let me take him." Charlie's crying seemed to slow down considerably when he saw Jack. He lifted his arms up and reached towards him.

Jack scooped him quickly out of the chair and held him close against his bare chest.

"It's okay, Charlie. Poor baby. We're going to fix you right up. You'll feel better in no time…."

His tone was deep and soothing. Rachel saw Charlie relax in Jack's arms and felt her own nerves soothed.

She felt better having Jack here to help her. A sick crying baby seemed to require eight arms working at once, to make things right again.

"Okay, just hold head still a minute so I can get this plunger thing in…" Rachel gave Charlie his medicine. The baby made a face for a moment but finally swallowed it.

"Success," Jack said, looking relieved.

"Now let's just hope he doesn't throw it up," Rachel was more experienced at these matters and knew it wasn't over yet.

"Did you call a doctor?" Jack balanced Charlie on his lap. The baby was tugging at his chest hair, but he didn't seem to notice.

"I am just about to. I'll get the service but hopefully, he'll call back." She filled a sippy cup with cool water and handed it to Jack. "See if he'll drink this. It will help bring the fever down."

Rachel called the service and left a message, including a list of Charlie's symptoms. It was hard when a child couldn't talk and tell you what hurt. Hard and scary. She didn't need a baby book to remind her that a high fever could mean anything.

She tried to keep calm and not let her imagination run away with her.

Jack was patiently helping Charlie with the sippy cup; half of the contents—or more—dripping down both of them.

"Okay, next thing we do is give him a bath. That will cool him down some."

Rachel went to take the baby, but Jack held on to him. "I've got him. You start the bath water running."

Rachel ran up to the bathroom and started the tub, testing

the water with her hand. She caught sight of herself in the mirror and gasped.

Her long curly hair flew around her head. Her eyes looked wild and her nightgown revealed...the works.

She had been so busy ogling Jack in the midst of her emergency, she hadn't given a thought to her lack of apparel.

A short wrap-around pink robe hung at the back of the bathroom door and she snatched it up and tied the belt just as Jack and Charlie came upstairs.

"The bath is ready. Let's put him in...."

Jack brought Charlie into the bathroom and they gently removed his sleeper and diaper. Then Rachel lowered him into his tub seat.

He normally loved a bath, but tonight his little face scrunched up and he started crying all over again.

"Poor Charlie...you don't feel very well, do you?"

Jack knelt down beside her, rubbing Charlie's small back with large, work roughened hand. They were side by side, so close she could feel his hip next to her own and his bare skin brush her arm.

She concentrated on soothing Charlie and wiping him all over with a wet wash cloth. His crying slowed, but never stopped entirely. It broke Rachel's heart to see him so distressed and she felt as if she was going to start crying too.

She sighed. "Okay...I think that's enough."

Her choked voice revealed her distress and Jack turned to her. He looked surprised a moment, then put his arm around her shoulder. "Don't worry, Rachel. It's probably nothing."

She nodded, knowing what he said was true. But she still felt bad for Charlie. "I just hate to see him sick. He must have felt sick all day...but I was so busy in the shop, I didn't notice."

Now she nearly did start crying, admitting her guilty feelings to him.

"Rachel, it's not your fault. Kids get sick all the time."

He hugged her close, so that her head was tucked against his shoulder.

"You're not…superwoman. Supermom. Super shop-keeper. You're a wonderful mother. Don't be so hard on yourself."

She sniffed and nodded. Just being close to him like this for a moment made her feel so much better. Recharged her failing batteries.

She lifted her head and glanced at him. "Let's get him out of the tub. I'll call the doctor again. He should have called back by now."

Jack lifted Charlie up and Rachel wrapped him in two soft towels, one with a little hood that covered his head. "I don't want him to get a chill now."

"He looks fine. Snug as a bug…I think he feels a little better." Jack said, cradling Charlie across his chest. "His body feels a lot cooler."

That was true. Rachel didn't need the thermometer to tell that Charlie's fever had gone down. She put on his diaper and some lighter pajamas, then handed him to Jack again.

"Just rock him a while. I think he might fall back asleep. I'll go call the service."

Rachel had to go down to the kitchen again. She didn't know the phone number of the doctor's answering service by heart and had been in such a panic when she'd called, she couldn't remember it.

Just as she reached the kitchen, the phone rang. It was Dr. Oakes, Charlie's pediatrician. "What's going on, Ms. Reilly? Charlie's not feeling well?"

"Thanks for the call, Dr. Oakes. Charlie woke up scream-ing with a really high temperature. A hundred and four…"

Rachel told the doctor what she'd done so far to make the baby comfortable, and answered his questions—rashes, vomiting, sneezing, coughing, runny nose…?

"Sounds like it might be an ear infection. Boys are prone. High fever. And he's rubbing his ear, you said."

"Yes, I noticed that."

"How does he seem now?"

"The fever seems to have gone down. I think he might fall asleep again."

The doctor said to keep giving him the fever reducing medicine and a lot of fluids.

"That's about all you can do for him tonight. Call me again if it seems worse. Otherwise, call the office first thing and bring him in."

"Yes, absolutely." She has to close the store for a while, but it couldn't be helped. Leaf peepers or not, she didn't even think twice about it.

As Rachel hung up the phone, she felt her body sag with relief. She'd been racing around on a shot of adrenaline and now felt herself suddenly crash.

She climbed the steps slowly, and approached Charlie's room.

She didn't hear him crying any more, or even that sad little snuffling sound he made sometimes instead when he was distressed.

She did hear Jack's voice, talking very softly, though his words were indistinct. She paused just outside the door. It was wrong perhaps to eavesdrop…but she couldn't help herself. She was…curious.

Was he telling the baby a story? At first it seemed so.

Then she realized, he was just talking to the baby. A random conversation. "…but you're going to the doctor tomorrow and you'll feel all better very soon. All you have to do is go to sleep now and have some happy dreams. Your Mommy loves you…and your Daddy loves you, too…."

Rachel took a step back into the dark hallway.

Had she heard that right?

Was Jack imagining he was Charlie's father? Maybe…

Maybe the entire emergency had gone to his head. Or maybe he felt bad for Charlie because the little boy didn't have a father.

And he was just trying to console him. Jack had grown up without his parents—mother or father—and knew what it was like to live with that loss.

Rachel took a breath. Had she been wrong to deprive Charlie of a father, of a "normal" upbringing? She'd made the decision very carefully before he was born. She knew it wasn't ideal, but she believed she could make up for the empty place in her child's life.

Lately at times, she wasn't so sure.

Rachel walked into the room and stood quietly a moment, taking in the sight of her child nestled in Jack's arm as he sat in a rocking chair by the window. Charlie looked so small and fragile. Jack looked so big and strong. But gentle and loving.

He looked up at her, finally realizing she was there.

She smiled and walked over to him. "Did he fall asleep yet?"

"Just about," Jack said softly. He stood up and carried Charlie over to the crib, then gently laid him down on the mattress.

"What did the doctor say?"

"Could be an ear infection. I need to bring Charlie to see him tomorrow."

"Yes, of course. I can take you," Jack offered.

Rachel glanced at him. "We'll see."

They stood side by side and gazed down at the sleeping child a moment. Rachel leaned over and felt his forehead. Cool.

The fever had broken, thank goodness. She stroked his hair a moment and stepped back.

"Let's let him sleep now. He's had a bad night."

"Tell me about it." Jack followed her out into the hallway.

She turned to him. "Thank you for coming over. Charlie's never been that sick before. I guess I was in a panic."

"You were great. You knew just what to do."

"It really took both of us to handle him. I'd still be trying to get the medicine thingy in his mouth."

Jack laughed quietly. "Maybe…"

Rachel felt suddenly self-conscious, standing with him in the darkened hallway, both of them barely dressed. She tugged at the belt of her robe, noticing the V-shaped opening in front was gaping open.

Jack looked as if he had noticed, too.

"So…how's the cottage? I didn't even get a chance to help you clean up in there today. Do you have everything you need?"

Her questions sounded forced and mechanical… Nervous, even to her own ears.

He didn't answer for a long moment, his gaze locked on hers.

"I do now," he said finally.

His voice was low and raspy, and Rachel felt as if every nerve ending in her body had been rubbed with rough velvet.

He stared down at her and sighed, his dark eyes growing smoky, wandering hungrily over her features. She discovered a thrilling light in his eyes, thrilling and terrifying. Jack wanted her. Wanted her in the worst way.

He slipped his hands around her waist and pulled her closer. Then he yanked the belt on her robe and it fell to the floor at her feet. Her breath caught at the back of her throat as his hands slipped under the fabric. She felt the heat of his palms on her skin, thorough her thin nightgown.

Rachel told herself to pull away. Step back, while you still have a chance.

But she was mesmerized by the smouldering light in his dark eyes, his face an unreadable mask.

A spark seemed to leap between them, like a bolt of lightening, lighting up the night sky. Her gaze dropped to his lips, and she felt herself weak with longing.

Her soft sigh seemed to push him over the edge. His head dropped and their lips met. This kiss was explosive.

Jack's mouth moved over hers hungrily and Rachel gave herself over to the wonderful pressure of his warm, firm lips on hers. His touch was commanding, confident. He urged her to follow and she eagerly responded. Her mouth opened against his like a flower and their tongues met in an intimate dance.

Rachel hardly knew herself, her hands wandering from his broad shoulders to his muscular back, her entire body rising into his embrace, yearning to feel more of his warm, strong body molded to her own.

"Rachel...sweet Rachel." Jack's head dropped to her shoulder, and he murmured her name against her bare skin, telegraphing a tingling sensation to every trembling limb.

He didn't need to say another. "Come into the bedroom," she whispered. "This way."

Their bodies were parted for barely a moment. Rachel let the robe slip from her shoulders. Jack pushed back the straps of her nightgown and pressed his hot mouth to her breast. First one, then the other. Her nipples had hardened to aching points and the touch of his lips felt electric. A hot molten wave of pleasure swept through her body. She clutched his head, aching to feel more of his caresses.

"God, you're beautiful. You really are," he whispered.

Rachel's mind was lost in a sensuous haze as Jack lifted her off her feet and carried her to the bed. At some point, her night gown had been tossed aside and she felt the cool air on her bare skin as she waited breathlessly for him to drop down beside her.

Her hands roamed hungrily over his body, stroking his long hard thighs and the hard ridge of his manhood that bulged beneath his jeans.

She tugged down his pants and slipped them off his long hard legs. He wasn't wearing anything more, as she had guessed. She stroked and teased him, driving him to the edge and felt a certain female power as she felt his big body shudder in her arms.

His hands stroked and caressed her, his fingers outlining the graceful curve of her thigh, then dipping into the warm, honeyed center of her womanhood.

He sighed against her mouth, then kissed her deeply, all the while gliding his fingers inside and outside of her. Wave upon wave of hot pleasure broke over her body.

Breathless and aroused to a fever pitch, Rachel felt about to explode.

Rachel had some experience with men, but had never responded like this. This was different. On another level entirely. It was as if their bodies were perfectly in tune, moving in a synchronized dance of pure pleasure, wordlessly. Effortlessly.

It was like making love in a dream. But this was no dream. It was hot and real and overwhelming.

With her hands on Jack's hips, she urged him to move over her. She lifted her head and pressed her lips to his chest, her tongue swirling around one flat male nipple. She felt him react, and heard him groan with delight. She fitted herself even closer, eager to feel him sink into her velvety heat.

Then she moved with him as he thrust himself inside of her.

The feeling was indescribable. Unbearably wonderful. She could barely stand it any longer and never wanted it to end.

Finally, her body arched with pleasure. She trembled and shook as brilliant lights exploded behind her eyes, reaching pleasure's peak.

Her head dropped limply back against the pillow and she gasped for air.

"My beauty…" Jack's mouth dipped down to her breast, his tongue twirling around her ultra sensitive nipple. "I'm not done with you yet," he whispered.

He slowly rocked inside of her, teasing and tempting, until she felt herself urging him on, and rising again to another astounding peak.

She gripped his shoulders and moaned, his hips bucking up to meet hers as he thrust deep inside of her.

Rachel closed her eyes and wrapped her slim legs even tighter around his waist. She matched his movements, rocking in a sensuous rhythm.

Higher and higher. Higher still.

Rachel felt herself shatter into a tiny, sparkling fragments. Like the afterglow of a giant cascade of fireworks. Almost at the very same moment, she felt Jack reach his own peak, in one powerful thrust, trembling for a long moment, then falling down into her arms.

They lay together without saying a word. She felt Jack's damp cheek on her shoulder and lifted her hand to stroke his hair.

He didn't move a muscle and she wondered if he'd fallen asleep. Finally, he lifted his head and stared down at her.

He slowly smiled and brushed a curly strand of hair back from her cheek.

"So…do you still think we're just friends?"

She would have thought he was serious, except for the teasing light in his dark eyes.

She tilted her head to one side on the pillow. "I guess we've moved to another category."

Though Rachel didn't know what that might be.

Chapter Seven

Rachel opened her eyes slowly. Beams of yellow sunlight slipped under the shade and she realized she'd overslept. She remembered Charlie was sick and began to sit up, eager to check on him. But just about the same moment, she realized she wasn't alone.

Jack's heavy arm was curled around her waist, his body tucked next to her own, spoon style, his dark head resting on the very same pillow.

Slowly and carefully, she slipped out from under his grasp. He stirred for a moment but didn't wake. Then, rolled to his back, bare to the waist down, a rumpled sheet clinging to his hips.

His thick dark lashes fanned out on his beard-shadowed cheek. His dark hair, mussed from sleeping, curled enticingly in every direction. He was a total bedhead, and easily the most attractive man she'd ever seen.

Images of their passionate lovemaking filled her head and Rachel had to turn away from the sight of him.

This was exactly what she didn't want to happen.

But just what she'd wanted, maybe from the moment he'd walked into her shop.

She picked her robe up from the floor, wrapped it around her naked body and headed for Charlie's room. He was awake, sitting up in his crib, playing with his white dog. He waved his arms and called out when he saw her.

She lifted him quickly and kissed his cheek, then checked his forehead. His skin was warmish, but not blazing hot like last night. She'd gotten up once during the night, she remembered now, to give him some fluids and medicine.

She carried him down to the kitchen and set him in his high chair, then fixed him a sippy cup of juice. Then she found the phone number for the pediatrician's office. The office wasn't open yet, a recording said. All she could do was a leave a message on the machine.

As she set about the task of making coffee, she thought of Jack, still asleep in her bed. A knot of morning-after-dread tightening in her stomach.

What now? What should she say?

"Oh, *blast*," she murmured. "What did I do?"

"Something wrong?"

Rachel turned quickly as Jack entered the room.

"I just spilled some coffee grains.... I hate when that happens."

He took a seat at the table and watched her, making her even more nervous. Bare-chested and barefoot, with his jeans hanging around his hips. Looking much the same as he had on her doorstep last night. Impossibly handsome.

I should have never let him in. That was the slip-up, right there.

"How's Charlie this morning?" He turned to the baby and touched his hand. "He looks a lot better."

"He still has a little fever, but he's gotten through the worst of it, I think."

The coffee had brewed and she filled two mugs.

"I'm just waiting for the doctor's office to call back so I can make an appointment."

"Is it far? I can take you there."

She brought the coffee to the table and set one down at Jack's place, then brought the milk and sugar over from the counter.

"The doctor is just in town. We can manage."

"All right. If you change your mind, let me know."

Rachel sat down across from him and sipped her coffee. She took a deep breath.

"Jack, I appreciate all your help. I don't know what I would have done last night if you weren't there...."

"You don't need to thank me so much, Rachel. I like to help you.... Let's just say it comes naturally. It's what I should do, that's all."

"Because you're a man and I'm a woman, you mean?"

He sat back, looking uneasy. "I didn't mean it that way.... Not entirely, anyway. It's hard to explain."

"Try me," she coaxed him.

He seemed to be thinking of some other reason he felt so protective and responsible towards her and Charlie. Some specific reason he either couldn't verbalize, or didn't want to.

He stared at her, suddenly looking very serious.

"Why does it bother you so much? Why shouldn't I help you?"

She sighed. Good point. *Because I'm falling for you, big time. Didn't you notice?*

"Because...it feels nice at the time. But we'll get too involved. I'll start to depend on you," she admitted.

"And that would be a bad thing?"

"Well...wouldn't it be? You told me yourself you love your freedom. After you finish the cottage where will you go next? I bet you don't even know."

"Of course I do," he argued with her.

Then he didn't say anything more.

He looked confused, upset, even a bit angry. Maybe she'd been too honest, too blunt. But that's how she saw it. If he wanted to convince her that he could be more stable, more serious relationship material, this was his chance.

But he didn't try, she noticed.

Finally, he sat back and crossed his arms over his broad chest. "You'd never get stuck on me, Rachel. You're as independent as the Statue of Liberty."

The comparison nearly made her laugh. But the conversation was too serious for that. Too important.

"Jack, last night was absolutely perfect. I wanted to be with you. I'd never deny that…."

"But?"

"Let's be adults about this. I'm not looking for anything serious…and neither are you…right?"

Her question hung in the air, her voice growing thin and tiny. Relaying her tiny, secret hope that he would finally argue with her. Insist that he'd been waiting for that one woman in the world who could make his heart sing and he'd found her, last night, in his arms.

That was the way she felt about him, deep in some secret place. Even if she could never admit out loud, or face it squarely.

"Are you talking about that being friends idea again, Rachel? It didn't really work for us the first time, you know?"

She felt herself blush. After last night, they could never jump back to that square on the game board. That was for sure.

"Of course not. I'm not that…unrealistic."

Her remark made him laugh. Even in his disheveled state— or maybe because of it—he was impossibly good-looking. A man didn't have a right to look that good at this hour in the morning.

"What do you have in mind? You don't seem to me like the type for anything but serious."

"Thanks a lot."

"I mean that as a compliment," he quickly replied.

"I can be casual. No expectations. No...recriminations. Afterward."

"After I'm gone, you mean?"

She nodded. "That's right."

"You sound very sure I will be."

She shrugged. So far, he hadn't said anything to make her think otherwise.

"Some man disappointed you. Who was it? An old boyfriend?"

Rachel's first impulse was to brush off the question. But then she decided he should know.

"I was engaged about two years ago. Everything was planned. Paid for. Even the honeymoon. I thought things were fine between us. Just goes to show how much you really know a person, right? But my fiancé broke it off at the last minute, a week before our wedding. So it was...sort of a shock."

To put it lightly. Not to mention the humiliation of it all.

Jack didn't say anything at first. "He had to be a fool to leave a woman like you. You're better off without a guy like that, Rachel. You know that, right?"

His instant disdain for Eric Rowland was comforting.

"Yes, I realize that. Now."

"But now you don't trust men, right?"

That question made her squirm. "I've found it best to just live my life, on my own terms, without waiting for anyone to make me happy or fulfilled. Isn't that your philosophy, Jack?"

Now he looked like he was starting to squirm. He wrapped both hands around his coffee cup, his dark brow wrinkled.

"I don't know what my philosophy of life is lately, Rachel. I certainly can't describe it this early in the morning. I haven't even finished my coffee."

He looked up and met her gaze. "If you want don't want to get into anything serious, fine. But I won't stop doing things for you and Charlie. I can't just turn that off."

"Fair enough. I'll put up with that part somehow. Nobody's perfect."

The corner of his mouth rose in a small smile. "You are, practically. As far as I can see."

Before she could argue about that too, he reached over and grabbed her shoulders, then kissed her, the firm pressure of his mouth waking every sleepy nerve ending in her body.

Jack pulled her deeper into the kiss, urging her up on her feet with their lips still locked. She wound her arms around his back and pressed herself against him. She could feel his body ready to make love all over again. And she felt herself melting in answer.

The phone rang, calling them both back to reality.

Rachel pulled away, too breathless and shaken to pick it up. The tone sounded and she listened for the message. It was the doctor's office, ready to make an appointment.

"I'd better call them back," she murmured.

"Yes, go ahead…I'd better go."

He slowly released her, took one more gulp of his coffee, then gave Charlie a loving stroke on his chubby cheek as he walked past the high chair.

While Rachel dialed with the doctor's office, Jack disappeared down the stairs and left the house through the back door. She watched him from the window, walking across the damp lawn.

She suddenly felt as if she'd woken up in another world, another life. It just all looked eerily the same.

Rachel had made an early appointment with the doctor. At first she planned to close the store, then had an idea. Lucy Martinelli, Julia's mother. She might be interested in watching the shop for a few hours. Lucy was a bit flaky and scattered, but Rachel had seen her in action at the fall fair and she got along great with customers.

When Rachel called and asked, Lucy was surprised but happy to help out. "I didn't have any plans for the day," she confessed. "I was thinking of trying the Singles Over Sixty luncheon at church. But that can wait until next week."

Rachel nearly laughed out loud. Julia would be pleased to hear Rachel had lured Lucy from that event.

When Lucy arrived, Rachel was dressed and ready for the doctor's appointment. She gave Lucy a few instructions about the shop and also left a written list of things that might come up and her cell phone number.

"Don't worry, dear. I'll be fine. If anything important comes up, I'll call you. Just take care of that little boy," Lucy added, gazing down fondly at Charlie.

"I will… Thanks again."

Rachel wasn't sure if Lucy could really handle the store. Especially if it got as hectic as it had been the day before. But it was better to stay open with somebody in there than to close, even for a few hours, in such a busy season.

When Rachel arrived at the doctor, she was relieved to see the waiting room empty. They were called almost immediately by the nurse and went into see Dr. Oakes.

As he'd suspected, Charlie had a middle ear infection and needed a prescription for antibiotics. Even though the visit was relatively brief, Charlie had been a handful, squirming and restless in his stroller and hard to keep amused while she waited in the exam room as the doctor and nurse went in and out, doing whatever it was they had to do.

She couldn't help but think how having Jack there would have made it easier for her. Certainly less tiring.

You never expected that having a child on your own would be easy, Rachel, she reminded herself. *Never mind about Jack. He'll spoil you with attention for the next two weeks, then disappear into the clear blue.*

She sighed. That was true. But it did promise to be an absolutely glorious two weeks ahead. If last night was any indication.

At the end of the visit, Charlie got a sticker and Rachel thought she deserved at least one, too.

Main Street looked busier than it usually did midweek. Rachel dropped off Charlie's prescription at the drugstore, then called Lucy.

"Everything's just fine, dear. I took a nice order for you. That pretty bed set with the appliqué ducks? The woman didn't want the matching bumpers, but I talked her into it."

Probably more likely that Lucy talked so much, the customer bought the bumpers just to escape.

But all in all, it made for a very nice sale. And more than made up for the cost of having a salesperson there.

"Great job. That is a nice sale. I should be back soon. I'm just waiting for a prescription."

"No rush. But if you could get back by noon, I'd appreciate it." Lucy's voice lowered to a near whisper. "There's a very nice gentleman here who's asked me out to lunch."

Leave it to Lucy. Rachel didn't know what it was she had, but she definitely had lots of it.

"Oh, I'll be back way before then."

"Thanks dear. See you."

Lucy hung up and Rachel wheeled the stroller down the street to Julia's office. Julia's car was parked in front so Rachel knew she had to be in.

She hoped Julia had a minute to chat. She had a lot to report.

She found her friend in the front office, looking at a computer screen with one of her salespeople. She jumped up and greeted Rachel and Charlie with a welcoming smile.

"What are you guys doing, wandering around town? Shouldn't you be at the shop?"

"Your Mom is watching the store for me."

"All the more reason," Julia said, looking surprised.

"Your mother is good with the customers, Julia. I was lucky she could come on such short notice. I had to bring Charlie to the doctor. He has an ear infection…."

"Oh, poor Charlie." Julia crouched down and stroked Charlie's cheek. "I hate it when he's sick."

"He had a horrific fever last night. I was terrified," she confessed. "The doctor said it's pretty common with boys. I'm just waiting to pick up a prescription at the drugstore."

Rachel was dying to tell her friend what else had happened last night. But they were surrounded by strangers.

Julia seemed to sense that something was up.

"Come back to my office," she suggested. "I've been running all morning. I could use a little break."

Rachel rolled the stroller back to Julia's office and Julia followed, then shut the door.

Julia had a spacious, sunny office, with a large desk, leather chairs set up in front and a separate sitting area with a couch and a work table, where she helped clients figure out mortgages and other real estate matters.

One wall was covered with plaques, recognition from all sorts of business associations for sales achievements, community service and achievements in her field.

Her friend was a professional success, no about it. Too bad some of that hadn't spilled over yet to Julia's social life.

Could a woman have it all? A successful career, a stable serious relationship, children…all the plates spinning at once? Rachel had always thought it was possible. But now she was starting to doubt it.

Maybe she should just be satisfied with what she could get. And a no-strings fling with a man like Jack was as good as it was ever going to get for her.

"You look unusually thoughtful this morning." Rachel sat on the leather sofa with Charlie's stroller parked beside her. Julia took a seat in a nearby arm chair. "Are you worried about Charlie?"

"He'll be okay once he starts the medication." Rachel handed Charlie a sippy cup of water and stroked his soft dark hair. She looked up at Julia. "Something else happened last night. With Jack."

Julia smiled and let out a long, "don't tell me" sort of sigh. "Well, that was inevitable, don't you think?"

"I didn't think it was inevitable. I still have this funny idea I have some control over my actions," Rachel said innocently.

"Rachel, you ought to see a video of the way you two look at each other. It was a done deal. Believe me."

Rachel sighed. "At least one of us isn't surprised."

"So...now what?"

"You're so smart. You tell me," Rachel challenged her.

Julia just laughed. "Did you talk to him this morning...or just leave it all hanging?"

"We did talk. I told him I didn't want to get involved in a serious relationship right now...and he didn't seem the serious relationship type either. And he didn't argue with me."

"Oh...okay. You don't sound so happy about that though."

"Well...he didn't argue with me. He didn't say he could even try to be more...stable."

"Maybe he knows he can't be," Julia looked at her. "At least he didn't lie to you."

"No, he didn't lie. But I would have felt better if he had," Rachel admitted. "At least I don't have any expectations. I do...have feelings for him though. That's the hard part."

Julia gazed at her sympathetically. "It's good to have feelings about someone, Rachel. I keep meeting men, very nice, acceptable men. And nothing clicks. I don't get that over-the-top feeling about any of them. I think you're really lucky to meet someone who just sweeps you off your feet and makes you feel as if you just can't help yourself. That doesn't happen too often in life," Julia's tone held a touch of sad knowledge. "Just see where it goes. Even if it doesn't work out perfectly. I don't think you'll regret it."

Hearing it put it that way, Rachel had to agree.

No one had ever made her feel quite the way Jack did. It was like watching a comet streak across the sky. It didn't last long. It wasn't meant to. But the ride was definitely worth it.

"Something to look back on in my old age?" Rachel said wistfully.

"Absolutely…and won't you have a big smile on your face, Granny," Julia teased her.

"If I forget, you remind me."

Men come and go, but friends like Julia were forever, Rachel thought.

Rachel suddenly remembered the time. "Thanks for the reality check. I'd better get back to the shop."

"Hope it's still there," Julia said blandly.

"Julia, you're way too hard on your mother. She has a talent for sales. She can talk to anyone."

"Rachel…let's not even go there."

Rachel just smiled in answer. She didn't want to go there, either. She certainly wasn't going to tell Julia that Lucy had a lunch date with one of the customers. She didn't want to get in the middle of the situation.

Rachel didn't see much of Jack all day. But when she closed the shop at 5:30 p.m., she went around back to the cottage. She could hear Jack inside, still working, running a table top saw. She stepped inside but he didn't hear her. He was looking down at the piece of wall board as the saw sliced through. His face was covered with dust and by plastic eye guards and a mask over his mouth.

Somehow, he still good. It was just…amazing.

She took a moment to gaze around the cottage. She'd seen the new roof, of course. But hadn't checked the progress inside for a few days.

The old tile ceiling had been torn down and the beams exposed. New wall board made the rooms look fresh and most of the work in the small kitchen had been completed as well.

It was really coming along. The realization cheered her. But also made her feel sad now, too. The sooner it was done, the sooner Jack would go.

Taking more than a piece of her heart with him now.

Jack lifted the saw and finally looked up at her. She could see him smile under the face mask. He pulled off his protective gear and walked over to greet her.

"Hey, Rachel. You were so busy in the store today, I didn't want to bother you. How did the doctor's visit go?"

"Charlie has to take some medicine but he'll be okay in a day or so. He was pretty frisky today. You'd never know he was so sick last night."

"Kids bounce back quickly."

"Looks like you've been busy too," she said, gazing around.

"I'm making good progress. Once I got that old roof off."

"Yeah…it looks great. When do you think it will be done?"

The question seemed so loaded now. Rachel struggled to keep a straight face.

"By the end of the month. As we agreed." Jacks' voice sounded a little curt, she thought. Maybe he was just tired. Or felt as she was nagging him. He turned his back and started to clean up the work area.

"Did you just stop by for a progress report?"

"No…" She walked over to him. Then put her hand on his back. "I wanted to see you…and find out if you want to come over for dinner."

She had gone back and forth in her mind today about the last part. But now that she was with him, she couldn't help herself. The invitation had just…come out.

Julia was right. You didn't feel this way about someone too many times in your life. She might as well enjoy it for as long as it lasted. And she could already count the days.

He turned, smiling slightly. "I'd love to have dinner with you. But why don't we walk into town and get a bite? You worked hard today, you don't have to cook for me again."

Rachel had to shake her head in wonder. Did this guy have a How To Be A Perfect Man script stashed away somewhere?

"Okay…how about pizza? There's a good place in town. Charlie loves it."

"Pizza it is then." She put her arms around his waist and he smiled down at her. "If I kiss you, you'll get all dusty," he warned.

"We'll just have to take a shower together."

His eyes lit up and she couldn't resist.

She lifted up on tiptoe and kissed him before he could say any other word.

Once Jack became part of her life, days and nights passed quickly, too quickly Rachel thought. Jack moved his belongings in from the cottage to her house and moved right into her heart as well.

They quickly worked out a daily routine, rising together early in the morning. Jack often took care of Charlie while Rachel made breakfast. Rachel would go down to the store at half-past eight and Jack would go out to work on the cottage.

They'd meet for a lunch break when Rachel wasn't swamped with customers, and then for dinner, cooking together or eating out at some easy, inexpensive place in town.

Jack never minded having Charlie along. In fact, he seemed to prefer it. He was a loving, attentive presence now in Charlie's life and Rachel began to worry that Charlie would be heartbroken, too, when Jack finally left.

Best of all, Rachel relished ending the day in Jack's arms. Making love endlessly, each time more spectacular than the last, each time more tender and wonderful. Making love to Jack she did things she'd never imagined. She reached heights of passion she thought only existed in romantic books and movies.

Rachel knew that it wasn't wise to lose herself so completely. But she couldn't stop herself. She realized that, for the very first time in her life, she was falling in love. Eric Rowland had been but a blip on her emotional screen. Jack Sawyer was...off the charts.

Whenever Rachel felt sad that their time together was ticking down, she'd push the thought out of her head and pretend that Jack was different—a steady, stick-around-type of guy that would stay with them forever.

Of course, Rachel knew that one day very soon she'd be forced to face the fact that Jack was anything but.

Chapter Eight

Seven glorious days later, Rachel was hit with an early, unexpected dose of reality.

She sat at the kitchen table, feeding Charlie his dinner—mashed hamburger, broccoli and a piece of roll with butter. Charlie seemed to like the butter the best and meticulously licked it off the bread.

Jack stood at the stove, cooking what he called his "Famous Flame-Eater Fireman's Chili."

With an apron tied around his waist and a towel slung over his shoulder, Rachel thought the chef himself looked mighty tasty. Never mind the chili. She could hardly keep her hands off him.

"Rice is done. And this chili looks about as good as it's going to get," he said finally.

He spooned some chili and rice into each of their plates, then sat down across from her at the table.

None of the men she'd known had ever cooked for her.

Not even Eric. She was determined to savor whatever Jack prepared. No matter what it tasted like.

"Smells great," she said encouragingly.

"Don't forget the cheese. It softens the assault on your taste buds."

Jack passed her a bowl of grated cheddar and she sprinkled her dish liberally.

"It can't be that bad, Jack. I love spicy food."

"So you've told me. Don't say I didn't warn you."

Rachel forked up a small bite and lifted it to her lips.

Jack was already eating. "Listen," he said between mouthfuls, "I need to tell to you something. I almost forgot. I'm having a little problem…."

She glanced at him. She could tell by now he was trying to sound off hand and natural, but a deep frown line on his forehead was a tell tale sign.

Did he need money?

She wouldn't be surprised, the way he'd been spending on her and Charlie lately. He never let her pay when they went out, or even share the bill. He couldn't pass a store without buying Charlie a surprise. The little boy's room was starting to fill up with toys and even sports equipment he wouldn't be able to use for years.

Charlie did like to teethe on the leather baseball glove, though.

"Do you need a payment or something for the work you've done so far? That wouldn't be a problem, Jack. I didn't even give you a deposit," she reminded him.

It was hard to tell for sure, but it looked as if he might have been blushing a bit under his tanned complexion.

"No, nothing like that," he assured her. "It's…another project of mine. Something's come up. I have to go check on this other thing. Just for the day. I should be back sometime tomorrow night."

She had just a fork full of chili in her mouth. As his words registered, she felt the food stick at the back of her throat. And lodge there. She didn't know what to do but swallow. But that made her cough.

She grabbed for a glass of water and felt Jack slapping her between the shoulders.

"Are you okay? I'm sorry.... Too spicy, right?"

She shook her head. "No...it's okay." She took a breath and then drank more water. "It just went down the wrong way. It's really very...tasty."

She actually hadn't noticed what it tasted like at all.

She knew Jack could tell she was putting on an act for him. Was he about to put one on for her? His famous disappearing act. Would one day away stretch out in three...or four? Was this his way of leaving for good? Where in the world did he go, anyway?

She felt him watching her carefully.

"Jack..." she began slowly. "I need to ask you a question."

"Okay. I'll answer it if I can."

Rachel waited a long silent moment. She carefully considered what she had to say to him and all the possible consequences.

Finally, she lifted her head and looked him in the eye.

"Did you put red pepper in this? Or was it just the chili powder?"

He looked relieved, but also disappointed. She wasn't sure why that should be, but there it was.

Did he want her to ask about his sudden secret trips?

If so, why didn't he just tell her what it was all about?

"Just the powder," he said finally. "I also toss in some fresh green chilies, chopped very fine."

"Oh. That makes sense." She nodded and started eating again.

He seemed to have some secret. Some other life. If he wanted to tell her about it, he would, she reasoned. The truth was, as close as they'd come, he was leaving here soon.

Maybe as soon as the end of next week. He'd said nothing so far to make her believe his plan was anything different.

It suddenly didn't seem right to question him, to pry. If he wanted to tell her, he would. In his own time. Or maybe, she'd never know.

For the past week they had created a perfect world between them, their own private paradise. It wouldn't last forever. The days left were precious and few. Why force herself out of this beautiful world any sooner than necessary?

The truth was, if Jack really had a secret, maybe she really didn't want to know.

They sat in silence for a few moments. Charlie cried out, slapping the top of his high chair. He'd been eating apple slices from a plastic bowl and now the entire contents flew onto the floor. Rachel started to rise, but Jack was faster.

"I'll get it." He picked up the fruit and bowl, tossed it in the sink and then wiped up the floor. Then he took another apple and started to fix a replacement.

"Rachel, is there something you'd like to ask me about? Other than my chili recipe?"

He stood at the counter and glanced at her for a moment over his shoulder.

Rachel was taken by surprise, but quickly recovered. "Such as?" she said mildly.

"Such as…where I'm going tomorrow. What I'm doing when I get there?"

"Well…do you really want to tell me, Jack?" She felt nervous and was sure he could hear it in her voice.

He gave Charlie his sliced apple and then sat at the table again. "Rachel…there are things you don't know about me."

She shrugged. "There are things you don't know about me. We don't know each other very long, do we?"

He shook his head, his gaze softening. "Maybe I don't know you very long, but I know all about you. There's a difference."

She understood his point. But what was all this leading up to?

A myriad of possibilities ran through her mind, none of them very good.

"Is this something bad? Should I be...afraid of you?"

She could hardly believe she'd asked such a silly question. He couldn't quite believe it either and couldn't help smiling at her now. He reached across the table and took her hand.

"No, it's nothing bad. You have absolutely nothing to fear from me. Ever. I'm not running from the law...and I don't have another relationship elsewhere, if that's what your thinking...."

Rachel let out a huge sigh of relief. She couldn't hide it.

"Well, that's good news. Listen, Jack, I don't think there's much you could tell me about yourself that would bother me. Let's just leave it at that, okay?"

He looked confused at her answer. About to argue with her.

As if on cue, Charlie tossed his bowl again, then watched the adults to see what they would do. Jack made a move to clean up the mess but Rachel touched his arm, stopping him.

"He thinks this is a game now. He thinks it's really funny."

Charlie laughed and clapped his hands, proving her point.

"He's a smart boy. He already has a sense of humor. You know they say humor is an important sign of intelligence."

Jack sounded so proud. You'd think Charlie was his own child. They were getting attached. Rachel worried about that. She thought Charlie would miss Jack almost as much as she would. Another reason not to get too serious about him.

She watched as Jack picked Charlie up and lifted him high above his head.

"You like that game better, buddy. Right?" Jack laughed with him.

Charlie squealed happily. He loved being tossed in the air. It must have felt like an amusement park ride to him, Rachel thought. It looked a little scary but she knew her baby was safe in Jack's strong embrace.

She wished she could say the same for her heart.

When they made love that night it felt somehow different to Rachel than all the other times before. Like a slow, sensuous dance. Endlessly seductive. Amazingly tender. Effortless and knowing.

Quiet passion smoldered between them, like the banked embers of a fire, intense at its core. A white-hot fire that could quickly flare up and burn out of control.

Jack's slow, masterful touch seemed to communicate more than desire or even a wish to give her pleasure. His hands and lips and mouth adored her. His whispered endearments thrilled her almost as much.

She surrendered herself to him, body and soul. And gave as good as she got. Alone in the dark, in their own special world, it was easy to physically express the feelings she had for him in her heart. Putting it into words, in the light of day, was the hard part.

She hated the idea of being apart from him for even a day. She couldn't bear to think about how she'd feel if it turned out to be any longer.

One day is bending you totally out of shape? What about forever? That's what you'll soon be facing, a little voice chided her.

Exhausted from their lovemaking, they fell limply into each others arms. She rested her cheek on Jack's chest, feeling his warmth surround her, his slow, steady breaths signaling that he'd fallen asleep. She forced herself to stay awake, listening to his heartbeat. She didn't want to waste a single moment of having him beside her.

When Rachel woke up the next morning, Jack's side of the bed was empty and cold. He'd slipped out of bed very early. She hadn't even heard him go.

She started her day feeling low-spirited, but Charlie's morning greeting and hug quickly improved her mood. His baby smiles were an instant boost to her brain chemistry. Even better than chocolate, Rachel had to admit.

The shop was very busy from the moment she opened the door. At the height of the customer rush—which was mainly a bus load of seniors from a ritzy assisted living facility in Connecticut—Rachel wished she had called Lucy Martinelli and had her helping again. As three well-coiffed grandma-types flashed their diamond and gold jewelry, vying for her attention, Rachel promised herself she'd call Lucy as soon as she had a chance. It would be great to have some help on the weekend.

It wasn't just the tour buses and blind luck that had increased sales. Rachel had to take some credit herself. She'd made up attractive advertising flyers with a discount coupon on the bottom. Jack had helped her with the computer graphics. She wasn't very good at that sort of thing but he seemed to know all about it. He claimed he needed it for his work though she wasn't sure how carpentry and home improvement dove-tailed with print shop software. But the brochure had come out looking very sophisticated and professional. So that's what counted.

She'd left Charlie with Jack for an hour or two one night while she roamed around the village, visiting shopkeepers, all the B & B's and even the manager of the Lion's Head Inn, if she could leave the brochures. Just about everyone had agreed and the coupons were already coming in, so she knew the simple marketing strategy had worked.

Her next target was the tour bus companies. She guessed that they made up some sort of packet for their customers. She'd contacted the largest tour company and sent a good pitch letter asking that her store flyer be included in their shopping guide. She had her fingers crossed.

She'd always worried that a romantic relationship would be a great distraction, a drain on her energy. But it seemed just the opposite with Jack. She felt like she could move mountains lately. Especially when he smiled at her a certain way.

It was late in the afternoon, while Charlie napped, that Rachel finally had a chance to look over her bookkeeping and tally up her sales for the week so far.

She had done surprisingly well, the best sales yet, and it was only Thursday. More tourists would be coming in over the weekend for sure. Tourists taking their autumn drives through the country.

She felt happy and relieved at the good news and wanted to share it with someone and celebrate. That made her feel even sadder that Jack wasn't around. She'd had no word from him all day and had no idea what time he would return—if he came back tonight at all.

The phone rang and she quickly picked it up, expecting to hear his voice. Her thoughts had magically reached him, reminding him to call in.

"Pretty Baby. Can I help you?" she answered in a professional voice.

"Rachel, it's me. Nora." Her sister's voice hung in the air between them for a long moment. Then her sister laughed nervously. "You remember me, right?"

"Nora…how are you?" Rachel didn't know what to say after that.

She hadn't spoken to her sister in over a year. There had never been a big, nasty fight. That would have been bad, but perhaps their situation was even worse. Their estrangement had built up slowly and steadily, the way a bricklayer builds a thick sturdy wall.

Still, Rachel wasn't really mad at her, just hurt. She was quite curious to hear why Nora was calling. Was she sick or in trouble? Rachel hoped not, but couldn't see why Nora would get in contact unless it was an emergency.

"I'm fine. Nothing really new to report," Nora's voice was

flat, with little expression. Especially when she got nervous, which she obviously was.

Almost like talking to a prerecorded announcement, Rachel had sometimes thought.

"Oh…that's good to hear," Rachel said.

"How are you, Rachel? How is…the baby? You named him Charlie, right?"

Rachel had to take a moment to compose herself. Was Nora actually asking after her nephew? After all this time? She'd never even seen him, her choice.

"Charlie's great. He's growing every day. He's almost a year old."

"Yes…I know. I remembered," Nora's voice sounded a little wistful. Or I am just imaging that? Rachel wondered.

"He's almost walking. He doesn't really talk yet, but has a few sounds that could be words."

"It sounds like he's growing up fast. I'm in New England on business. I'd like to see him. And you of course," she added with another nervous laugh. "I can be there tomorrow sometime. Does that work out for you?"

"Tomorrow?" Rachel felt her head spin. She'd been too busy to eat lunch and this entire conversation was a shock.

"Sorry for the short notice. I was nervous about calling you," Nora admitted. "Would you rather I didn't come, Rachel?"

Maybe some other time would have been more convenient. When they had time to plan?

Rachel didn't think any time would be ideal to face her sister. "I'm surprised by your call, Nora. But I think you should come. I think that's a good idea."

The bell on the shop door rang and Julia walked in. Rachel guessed from her outfit that she'd either had an important meeting somewhere or had been to a special closing. She wore a tailored, dove gray suit with a fine, chalk-line pin stripe. The French blue tailored shirt underneath brought out Julia's fair coloring and eyes perfectly.

Rachel had never been so glad to see a friend in her life.

She signaled to Julia that she'd be off the phone in a minute and then finished up with her sister, giving her driving directions to Blue Lake and her shop.

When she hung up, she still felt stunned.

"Busy day? You look exhausted."

"I'm probably a little pale. I've just seen a ghost.... Actually, just got a phone call from one."

Julia frowned. "Not your ex-fiancé? They do have a way of coming out of the woodwork when you're finally happy. It's sense of smell or something."

"No, not Eric. Thank goodness." That was all she needed. "My long-lost sister, Nora. Who basically told me to get lost when I decided to have Charlie and never wished me well or good luck or any of those things when I left the city and came up here."

"Oh, that Nora. The Toxic Sister. I remember her now." Julia nodded and dumped her big purse on the counter top.

"She's in New England on business. She's stopping here tomorrow. Sort of a sneak attack."

"Did she say why she wanted to come after all this time?"

"Not really. She sounds like she wants to see Charlie. I guess that's why I want her to come too. She always expected me to end up alone and penniless, with Charlie depending on me," Rachel added. "Maybe she got worried that her prediction came true and her conscience is bothering her."

"Won't you be proud when she finds out she was totally wrong?"

Rachel had never been the gloating type. But she knew she would take some satisfaction in showing Nora what a good life she'd made for herself and Charlie up here.

"The trouble with Nora is that the glass is not just half empty. It's also chipped. I think things are working out fine. I know I'm not a millionaire. Yet. But the shop is off to a strong start. That's something. But Nora won't see any of that," she added.

"She sounds like fun. How long is she staying?"

"I was so surprised to hear from her, I forgot to ask," Rachel realized. "Guess I'd better be prepared if she expects to stay overnight."

Julia picked up a tiny, hand-knit cardigan. It was pink with heart-shaped buttons and a pattern of hearts in all different colors around the collar and lower hem. Rachel guessed by the way Julia handled it she was having a bout of baby longing again, but decided not to ask her about it. Unless she wanted to bring it up herself, of course.

"What about Jack?" Julia asked, suddenly folding the sweater and putting it down where she'd found it.

"Good question. I have to banish him back to the cottage. I know it sounds cowardly, but I don't want to give Nora all that ammunition. I can just imagine what she'd say if she found out he's living here...and we hardly know each other...and there's no future in it."

"If she has eyes in her head, she'd say, 'You lucky, lucky girl.'"

Rachel grinned. "Aren't I, though?...but that's not how Nora would see it."

"She sounds like your complete opposite," Julia cast her a warm smile. Rachel was grateful for the compliment.

"So, speaking of Jack, what's going on? Your message was a little vague. Did you guys have an argument?"

Rachel had left Julia a message on her cell saying only that something had happened and call if you have a chance.

"No, not exactly. Last night at dinner he told me he needed to take a day off and take care of one his mysterious emergencies. He said he'd be back tonight. But so far, he hasn't even called."

"Did you ask him any questions? What it was all about?"

"At first I did. He was sort of evasive. Then later it seemed like he did want to tell me but…I chickened out." Rachel glanced up at Julia. She was embarrassed to admit it, but Julia was her best friend. She knew she could tell her anything.

"What does it really matter? He's not going to be here very much longer. I guess I just didn't want to spoil what little time we have left." She paused and sighed.

"Fair enough," Julia looked at Rachel with concern. She reached over and patted Rachel's hand. "Jack is a good guy. A little eccentric maybe. But whatever his secret missions are about, I don't think it can be anything really awful."

"I don't think so, either," Rachel agreed. "If he doesn't want to tell me, I'm not going to interrogate him about it, either. He claims there are emergencies with other work projects. I know it sounds flimsy but…I'm going to just trust him. And let it go."

Julia nodded in a reassuring way, but before she could speak the phone rang. Rachel picked it up and answered with her shop keeper's greeting.

"Rachel? Glad I caught you," Jack greeted her.

She could tell he was calling from a cell phone, a static sound crackling in the background.

"Jack…." *Where are you?* She was about to say. But caught herself just in time.

"Are you on your way back?" she asked instead. "I can wait to have dinner with you."

"Sorry, babe. I'm not able to get back tonight. The situation is a little more complicated than I expected. I'll be back tomorrow for sure, sometime around noon," he promised.

"Oh…okay," Rachel said dully. She had to admit, she really wasn't surprised. Disappointed, but not surprised.

"Everything okay?" His voice held a note of concern. "Charlie is okay, I hope?"

"Charlie is fine. He misses you," Rachel answered honestly. *I do, too,* she thought, but didn't say.

Jack chuckled warmly. "I miss him too. I miss you both."

His simple words warmed her heart. She suddenly ached to hold him.

"I miss you, too, Jack," she said in a low voice.

"What? I'm sorry, honey. I can't hear you. The reception is breaking up."

"I said...oh, never mind." Rachel sighed. "Listen, my sister is coming to visit tomorrow. She just called."

"What? Call you tomorrow? Okay, I'll be on the road though."

"My sister. She's coming to visit. Nora. Remember I told you about her? I need to move your things back into the cottage."

"Rachel...I'll get back to work on the cottage right away. Don't worry."

"That's not what I said, Jack."

The static sound filled the space between them. Finally, Rachel heard Jack's voice again.

"I can't hear a word you're saying. Sorry. I'm going to hang up now. Take care, okay?"

Rachel heard Jack disconnect the call and she hung up, too. Julia had wandered over to the far side of the shop, politely giving Rachel some privacy. She now wandered back and took a seat on a stool near the counter.

"He's not coming back tonight. Tomorrow, he said. Around noon."

Julia didn't say anything for a moment. Then she said, "Want to hang out here and order pizza or something? I'll run up to the video store and get a movie. Something sappy and romantic?"

"Sounds perfect. I can use a break from 'Best of Elmo.' We watch it almost every night."

"Great. What do you want on the pizza?" Julia asked as she grabbed her car keys.

"Oh, blast. I just remembered. I have to get ready for Nora. I have to move all Jack's stuff, clean the apartment, do some wash. I don't think I have any clean sheets or towels...and I have to get some food in the house. Isn't that Super Shop in Winston open twenty-four hours?"

"Slow down, pal." Rachel held her hand up like a traffic cop. "First of all, your sister has snubbed you for years. I don't think you need to make yourself crazy and treat her like a member of the royal family."

Rachel started to interrupt, but Julia held the floor.

"Second, I have absolutely nothing to do tonight but avoid phone calls from Stew Kramer."

"You reached your three date limit...at date two?"

"One and a half. We did coffee on Tuesday. Anyway, I'll pick up some take out, change my clothes and grab my new vacuum. If we clean up your place together, we'll still have time for that sappy movie...what do you think?"

"That you're the greatest friend in the world." Rachel replied honestly. "You get to pick the movie."

"Deal." Julia smiled briefly and grabbed her purse. "Be back in say...half an hour."

Julia grabbed her bag and swung out of the shop. Rachel picked up Charlie from his play pen and took him upstairs. She quickly fed Charlie and ran his bath. He had skipped a nap and she expected him to fall asleep easily. He was such a deep sleeper, once he fell asleep even the sound of a vacuum wouldn't disturb him.

As she quickly washed Charlie, she felt her energy fading. She normally would have refused Julia's offer of help simply on principle. But now she was glad her friend was coming back.

Maybe Jack had taught her that it was okay to accept these simple gifts offered by people who cared about her. She knew that at somewhere down the road, she'd pay Julia back for the favor.

Besides, it would be nice to have Julia around. She couldn't help worry about seeing Nora tomorrow, and couldn't help wondering where Jack was spending the night.

It was hard to be a single parent with a ten-month-old baby who played in every single room, run a business and keep a perfect house.

It was actually impossible, Rachel decided. Impossible for her anyway. She accepted the fact that the standards she'd had for her immaculate and beautifully decorated apartment in Manhattan no longer applied. The new rules included a decor that blended with giant plastic toys, play mats and piles of stuffed animals.

"Your kids won't remember that the house was clean," a very wise woman had once told her. "They'll remember that you played with them, made cookies, read them a story."

Rachel had taken that advice to heart and preferred any of those activities to cleaning anyway, so it worked out.

She'd been so busy in the shop the past few days, she hadn't been able to play with Charlie much…or clean up. Jack was tidy and helped her pick up at the end of the day. But the mess had compounded somehow and everything looked out of place, sort of left wherever it landed to be rooted out as needed.

Rachel took a big laundry basket and started to gather the miscellaneous objects that trailed from room to room.

Julia returned and called up from the back door a short while later. "Okay, come on up, but it isn't pretty," Rachel warned her.

She heard Julia scoff, then when she reached the top of the stairs and looked around, she did look a bit daunted.

"You sure you haven't been robbed? It looks almost… ransacked."

Rachel glanced at her. "You're sure you want to spend a free evening here? It's not too late to back out. I'd totally understand."

"Come on. It's just…stuff. It won't take long."

Julia sprang into action, helping Rachel get a second wind. Julia was a whirlwind, moving with the same speed and efficiency she applied in her office. Rachel was amazed at how quickly the place started to shape up. Her two-story apartment was actually a lovely space and nicely decorated. Minus the baby equipment. It was homey and cozy, with artistic touches— pillows and curtains she'd made by hand in the living room and bedroom. Charlie's room was especially enchanting, decorated in white and ocean blue, with one of her own murals painted on the largest wall—a bunny family picnic.

No, she didn't have anything to be ashamed of here, she thought. Though Nora would doubtlessly find some fault with the age of the house, the slightly crooked floor in the hallway, the old kitchen cabinets that she'd painted pure white and stenciled with an ivy vine pattern.

After all the rooms were cleaned and fresh sheets put on the bed, Julia and Rachel packed up Jack's belongings and carried them out to the cottage. There wasn't much, but it was all very telling. If Nora so much as found a men's razor or one of Jack's socks in the bedroom, it would open up an entire can of worms.

They stumbled over the lawn, entered the cottage and flicked on the lights. Rachel had seen the progress day by day, but Julia was shocked at the transformation.

"Wow! This place looks…awesome." She twirled around, gazing up at the skylights and vaulted ceiling, then walked over to check out the updated kitchen.

"The guy's a genius. I can't believe he did all this by himself…" She looked up Rachel. "What did he charge you again?"

Rachel told her the figure and Julia shook her head.

"He definitely underbid this job, Rachel. I can't imagine he could even buy all the supplies for that figure." Then seeing Rachel's look of dismay, she added, "But these guys always have connections for discounts and loads of material left over from other jobs. Hey, you got a great deal. He probably just needed the work and didn't want to scare you off."

He had said he needed the work. That had to be it. What other explanation could there be? "I hate to think I've taken advantage of him. Do you think I should give him a bonus or something?"

Julia smiled. "I think you've taken care of that, dear," she said tartly.

Rachel felt herself blush. "Julia. You know what I mean...."

Julia patted her arm. "Talk to him about it when he's finished. He may have underbid. It's extremely unusual for a customer to offer to pay more on a contract. They're usually complaining about something and want to pay less."

"I know that," Rachel said, rolling her eyes.

"But considering your unusual relationship with your contractor, he might appreciate it."

Julia gazed around again. Rachel could almost hear the wheels turning in her head. "I can rent this place in a second. Figure out the utility cost and we'll come up with a good figure."

Rachel liked that news, though since business had picked up so much the past week or so, she didn't feel nearly as pressured about money.

After careful consideration of what to take and what to leave, they made one trip back to the cottage with a load of Charlie's excess toys. Nora would probably only be around for a day or so, Rachel figured, and Charlie wouldn't miss some of things for that short a time. It did make the apartment look larger and neater once they were gone.

Just as Julia had promised, before too long, they were lounging around Rachel's living room, watching a sweeping drama about lovers parted by misunderstandings, and the ill-spirited intentions of a jealous friend. When the couple is finally reunited, the heroine is nearly dying, but her long-lost lover risks his life to save her, and nearly loses his own.

Rachel could only think of how Jack would have squirmed through every minute of it. Or would have been inspired by the love scenes to coax her into the bedroom and have one of their own.

Not that she didn't think about him every second of the film. Of course she did.

But it was good to have a woman pal like Julia. There were some things a guy just didn't get.

Chapter Nine

Waiting for Nora to arrive, Rachel was as jumpy as a grass-hopper on a hot griddle. Despite the fact that she'd cleaned for hours and stayed up late with Julia the night before, she sprang out of bed at half past six, taking great pains with her appearance and with Charlie's, so that they'd both look their very best.

A steady flow of customers during the early morning was some distraction. Finally, at about ten, Nora called from the road. She'd reached town but was having trouble finding Rachel's address. It sounded as if she'd driven in the wrong direction up Main Street.

Rachel turned her around, hung up the phone. Then she panicked.

Luckily, the shop was empty. She took a few deep breaths, then picked Charlie up from his play mat and cleaned his face and hands with a wipe, then smoothed out his hair.

His adorable outfit—red overalls and a striped turtle neck patterned with bears, striped sox and patent leather boots—

looked rumpled but wasn't stained. He'd also lost one shoe, which she couldn't find for the life of her. She decided she didn't have time to change him or find new shoes, so she removed the one that remained.

Charlie lifted his hand and grabbed her nose. She started down at him and caught herself. Charlie was a wonder. In a clean outfit, or a dirty outfit. With shoes or without.

"If she doesn't think you're perfect, who needs her?" Rachel whispered.

Charlie laughed and grabbed at her nose again. He definitely agreed.

"Rachel…? I'm here," Nora paused in the doorway to slip off her large sunglasses and look around. Finally she smiled.

She looked nervous, Rachel thought, though very much the same.

Nora was petite and slim, with straight shiny hair, parted on the side and cut to her chin. She was dressed all in black— "practical for traveling" Rachel was sure Nora would say. Black pants and boots with a belted cardigan under a light black top coat that came to her knee. A dash of bright red lipstick contrasted with her pale complexion and dark hair.

Rachel walked over and hugged her sister. Nora stood stiffly, but seemed to make some small effort.

"So, you made it. Good to see you." Rachel stepped back and smiled.

It was good to see her. For all their differences, Nora was still her sister, the only sibling she had. Rachel was sure that if their mother was still alive she would have been distressed by her daughters' falling out.

"Good to see you, too, Rachel." Nora gazed at Rachel from head to toe. "You look…healthy. Are you breast feeding?"

Rachel thought that was a nosey question to ask, all things considered. "I did. But I'm not any more."

"Oh…" Nora's mouth formed a small circle. Then she shut it. "Well…you do look like this place agrees with you."

Rachel could tell what Nora meant by that remark. Women who are breast feeding usually don't lose much of their pregnancy weight. She knew she wasn't as slim as she'd been while living in New York. She didn't need Nora to tell her that.

Nora was very weight conscious, though her metabolism kept her naturally skinny. She had no idea how some people struggled just to drop a pound or two but felt herself superior, just because she was thin.

"It does agree with me," Rachel said curtly.

Nora followed her into the shop. "Where's Charlie? I'm dying to see him."

Which is why you waited nearly a year?

"I have a nursery and a playroom for him down here," Rachel explained. "I'll get him."

Rachel went into the nursery, then bent over Charlie's Portacrib. He hadn't done much damage in the two minutes he'd been sitting there alone.

"Okay, kid. It's show time," she whispered.

She lifted Charlie up and carried him out, turning him to Nora's view.

She saw her sister's thin, sour expression light up. As much as Nora's expression ever did.

"Oh my…isn't he cute." She glanced up Rachel. "He doesn't look much like you, Ray," she said bluntly. "I guess he takes after his father. No way of knowing, of course.…"

Rachel was about to snap back with a short tempered reply, then caught herself. How long had Nora been there? Less than five minutes? And she'd already gotten off a pretty good insult.

A new record, even for her.

Charlie waved at her, but she didn't seem to notice. She'd already lost interest in him and was looking around the shop.

"This is a pretty old house. Did it cost you much?"

"No, it was a real bargain. I had to do some repairs and renovation. We live upstairs in an apartment. There's a cottage out back. I'm going to rent it. When it's fixed up."

"These old houses, they're money traps, aren't they? I'd bet it would have cost just as much to knock it down and start from scratch."

Knock it down? This beautiful old Victorian? The thought would never have crossed Rachel's mind, even if the house had been in terrible shape. Which had not been the case.

As an accountant, Nora was skilled with handling money. She never made an emotional or impulsive spending decision. If she'd bought this property, the decision to let the house stand or knock it down would have been based purely on dollars and cents.

"I went over the math pretty carefully. It was worth the investment," Rachel assured her sister.

"I hope so. For your sake," Nora said with concern. "How's the real estate market around here?"

"Oh, it's strong. Lots of second home buyers. My closest friend is a Realtor," Rachel added.

"Good. She can probably find a quick sale…if you ever had an emergency." Nora nodded, as if she was just trying to give some helpful advice.

She picked up a baby quilt with satin trim, then glanced at price tag. "My, my…people will pay that much for a tiny little blanket?"

"It's an original. One of kind," Rachel explained. "It takes time to put a quilt together, even though it's not very big. To coordinate the patterns and colors…"

"I see." Nora looked around, seeming bored by the explanation. "Nice music," she remarked, noticing the classical music that played in the background. "Very relaxing. It's so quiet in here. I guess it's much less stress than your real job. I mean, your job in New York."

"It's just quiet right now. The shop has been very busy, especially on the weekends."

Rachel did not mean to sound defensive, but it was hard to keep a certain edge out of her tone.

"I'm sure you do, Rachel. Don't be upset. Why are you so sensitive?" she asked with an innocent tone. "I'm just trying get some idea of your life these days, that's all."

Nora touched her arm in a conciliatory gesture, then chucked Charlie under the chin. He never liked when grown ups did that. He batted her hand away.

"The baby's not very social, is he? Is he afraid of strangers?"

Rachel sighed and shook her head. "Not usually."

Charlie was the friendliest baby in town. Everybody knew that. It just went to show, Nora could bring out the worst in anyone.

Rachel heard Jack's truck roar up the driveway and she felt her body grow tense. After their jumbled conversations last night, she'd never gotten a chance to speak to him. To explain about her sister's visit.

She hoped she could get him alone for a moment, before Nora got the wrong idea. Well, the right idea, actually. The one Rachel knew she'd frown upon.

Maybe he'd go to the cottage and start working. But no, he strode up the walkway to the store, looking like he owned the place.

He flung open the shop door and greeted Rachel with a wide, warm smile. He was wearing a leather jacket she'd never seen before; it looked very expensive. Another purchase beyond his means, she thought.

Other than that, he looked pretty much the same, wearing a burgundy colored sweater under the jacket, worn jeans and work boots. The same tall, dark gorgeous hunk of manhood who had been driving her crazy for weeks.

She wanted to run across the shop and fling herself into his arms…and then drag him back into the store room. The gleam in his dark eyes told her he felt the same.

But of course, Nora was watching and she would feel awkward even giving him a peck on the cheek.

"Jack, this is my sister, Nora. She was up here on business in New England and decided to visit."

"Good to meet you, Nora." Jack stepped forward and stretched out his hand, flashing his most charming smile. "Jack Sawyer. I'm—"

"—the contractor who's renovating the cottage." Rachel cut him off. She had no idea how he might describe himself or their relationship. And didn't want to find out.

"It's a nice space but needed a new roof and some other repairs," Rachel explained to her sister. "I'm going to rent it out."

"Oh, right. Good idea." Nora nodded. "You could probably use the extra income. I mean, with business being so slow. Too bad you're at the end of the street. You have some pretty things in here, but it's hard to find."

Rachel had never said that business was slow. She'd told Nora just the opposite. But that was Nora for you, her ideas and opinions were usually set. It didn't really matter what you said, or even what she saw with her own eyes.

Rachel didn't even bother to correct her.

Jack laughed. "Don't worry, they find her. Sometimes the place gets so crowded you'd think she was giving something away."

"Really? I'd wait to see that." Nora's tone was sarcastic.

She was a snob and obviously didn't like being corrected by the handyman.

Jack looked at Rachel. "Is she for real?" his expression seemed to say.

Rachel met his gaze but didn't glance back. She was touched by the way he defended her. But she didn't want any more head butting between Jack and her sister. She had her own issues with Nora to iron out.

"So, Nora…how long can you visit? I forgot to ask."

"Oh, just for the afternoon. I'd love to stay longer. It was hard to find a room in town last minute. Can you imagine that? I thought, a little nowhere place like this, of course I could find a room easily. But every bed and breakfast is full. And there aren't many choices."

"It's the Leaf Peepers," Jack explained. "They're everywhere."

His expression was serious but Rachel was sure he was teasing. Trying to alarm her.

Nora gave him a puzzled look. "The...what?"

"Leaf peepers. Tourists who come to see the foliage," Rachel explained. "Would you like to stay over? You can have dinner with us and have a little more time with Charlie."

"That's a nice invitation, Rachel...but I don't want to put you out."

"It's no trouble, honestly," Rachel replied. *You're only putting Jack out. Back out into the cottage.*

"Well, thanks. I'd love to stay." Rachel could tell her sister was touched and genuinely appreciated Rachel's hospitality. She probably realized she didn't deserve it.

"Great. Come upstairs and I'll show you the rest of the house. We can bring up your bags."

"I only have a small overnight bag. Out in the car." Nora glanced at Jack as if she expected he might offer to get it for her.

Jack just smiled and crossed his arms over his chest. "It's good to travel light. I wish I had the knack."

Nora nodded. "I'll just run out and get it," she said, then left for her car.

The bell on the closing shop door seemed to signal the start of a race.

Jack grabbed Rachel, pulled her into the nursery room, then quickly but carefully lifted Charlie and put him in his playpen. In one swift motion he wound his arm around her, pulled her close and tight, and kissed her so hard and long, she felt her legs go weak.

She struggled for a moment, not because she didn't want to kiss him. She just wanted to tell him about Nora.

But he wouldn't abide any verbal communication. He

smothered her face and mouth with hot, hungry kisses, his lips and tongue trailing down her neck into the deep V-neck-line of her T-shirt.

"Miss me?" he murmured against the soft skin at the top of her bra. "I missed you…"

"You know I did.…" Rachel's words were ragged with desire, the nipples on her breast growing achingly taut as his hand moved over her shirt.

She felt Jack's hard body pressed against her own and closed her eyes, imagining they were alone in her bedroom and had all the hours they'd lost last night to make love.

The bell on the shop door rang, an abrupt signal to the end of their private time. Rachel was sharply jolted back to reality. She pulled away and took a deep, settling breath.

"I'll be right out," Rachel called. She looked down at her clothes, then hurriedly straightened her T-shirt and bra.

Jack turned away to tuck in his shirt and smoothed his hair with his hands.

"That's your sister?" His voice was a husky whisper. "Are you sure? You're nothing alike. You don't even look alike."

"Yes, that's my sister. I'm glad she came. I know she's not exactly warm and cuddly, or the life of the party but—"

"Not exactly, no. None of the above."

"—but she's all the family I have. We have some differences to work out. So I need to try to patch things up."

Jack's expression turned serious. "Okay, enough said. I'm sorry I teased her. What can I do to help?"

Rachel sighed and looked away from his soft brown gaze.

"For one thing, I don't think it's a great idea if she finds out you're living in the apartment. That will get her off on a whole new list of things wrong with my life…"

"Oh, thanks a lot."

Was he genuinely hurt, or just being sarcastic? She couldn't tell for sure.

"Jack, it's just the way it will look to her. She's very con-

ventional. Very...judgmental. You and I know each for what...
three weeks? We have no commitment, no plan for the
future..."

"I get your point," he said tightly.

Rachel didn't understand why he was upset. It wasn't as
if they hadn't talked about all this before. Wasn't that the way
he wanted things to be between them?

"What's the bottom line here? Am I allowed to call you
by your first name?"

"The bottom line is, your belongings are in the cottage. For
tonight. We act as if...as if we've just gone a date or two.
That's what I'll tell her."

It seemed too silly to pretend that she and Jack had no
personal relationship. She didn't think they could even
manage it. But Nora didn't have to know the whole story.
Rachel just wanted to avoid her prying questions and re-
crimination. She had enough trouble dealing with Nora's dis-
approval of Charlie and her path to motherhood.

But Jack didn't know about any of that.

Jack shook his head. She thought he was going to start
arguing with her again. Then he met her gaze.

"All right. I'll go along with this. But I'm doing it for one
reason, Rachel. I can see how much this means to you and...
I..."

"Yes?" She waited, wondering what else it was he
wanted to say.

"I...I care for you."

"Oh...thanks."

He cared for her. Well, that was something. It wasn't what
she wished he would say. It wasn't as if he'd said, "I love you."
"I care for you" was the default phrase men used to avoid
saying "I love you." Men who wanted to avoid...everything.

She had a feeling that wasn't what he started to say. But
she didn't have time to decipher his mood and hidden
meanings. That could take a lifetime.

She scooped up Charlie and headed for the door. She and Nora had a lot to catch up on.

Rachel thought Nora would get bored in the shop, but her sister didn't seem to mind visiting while Rachel waited on a few customers who came in. Rachel felt as if she was on stage, under her sister's scrutinizing eye. But by now she could play the part of the friendly, knowledgeable shopkeeper in her sleep and each of the customers bought or ordered merchandise.

It wasn't a stampede but still proved to Nora she was making a living.

During the down time, Nora asked how Rachel had chosen the town and found the property. Pretty much by accident, Rachel had to admit.

"But it all worked out for the best. It's a great place to live."

"Do you have any regrets about leaving New York? You gave up a good job, real security," Nora reminded her.

"No, none at all. I'm really happy here. Really, Nora," she repeated.

Nora gazed at her, seeming unconvinced. "I sometimes thought you were being impulsive, Rachel. Just overreacting to the way Eric treated you. I sometimes wonder if you waited a few months, gave yourself some time to think things through more, if you would have made the same choices."

Rachel had to admit that Nora had a point. She'd often wondered the same thing herself.

"I did what I thought was best for me, Nora," she answered finally. "I can't say that being left at the altar had nothing at all to do with my choices afterward. But I do think I made the right ones. For me."

Nora sighed and gave Rachel another of her long considering looks. "If you say so, Ray."

Rachel could tell her sister was not totally convinced, but seemed willing to drop the subject.

At noon, Rachel encouraged Nora to take a break from the store, and walk into town for lunch.

"I guess I'd like to see the village," Nora said, slipping on her slim black coat. "What about you? Aren't you hungry?"

"I'll just grab a yogurt or something from the kitchen and eat down here. I don't like to close midday."

That wasn't entirely true. Rachel did sometimes close for an half hour or so when the shop was slow. But she needed a break from Nora and thought it would be good for her sister to see some of Blue Lake. It was rare to meet anyone who didn't fall under the spell of the quaint shops and buildings and beautiful village green.

Rachel was soon glad she had not closed the store. She'd just fed Charlie and put him down for a nap when a wave of customers arrived. An actual parade of seniors, traveling in a group, with cameras and camcorders hanging from their necks, sun visors and tote bags.

When Nora returned, she could hardly get in the store.

"For goodness sake! Where did they come from? It looks as if a bus just pulled up."

"Actually, a bus did pull up. I've been working with a tour company, to get on their list of stops. I didn't think it was going to start so soon, though."

Nora turned to her. "You'd better hire some help. Good service is important, especially at these prices."

Funny how her sister had gone from advising on an emergency exit plan for a failing business, to advice on hiring more employees

"Would you mind helping me this afternoon, just a little?" Rachel coaxed her.

"Me?…I don't even know where anything is."

"If you have any questions, I'm right here. You'd be surprised at how many people know just what they want," Rachel added. "You really don't need to say that much."

Before Nora could argue or escape, a customer walked up to her holding out a holiday dress of burgundy velvet with smocking on the bodice, satin ribbon trim and a lace color.

"Miss, is this machine washable?" the customer asked.

Nora looked appalled at the question. "These are hand-made, one of kind, fashion originals. This smocking is all done by hand. Of course they're not machine washable."

She snatched the dress out of the woman's hand, as if she didn't deserve to handle it.

"Yes…it is beautiful. I thought so, but I wanted to ask… I'll take it."

Nora lifted her chin. "Will that be cash or charge?"

Wow, Rachel thought. *She's a natural.*

At dinner that night, they had something to laugh about together. A rare occurrence in all their years of sisterhood.

Well, as adults perhaps.

Jack joined them for dinner also, and managed to stick to the agreement. He didn't argue with Nora, no matter what she said, for which Rachel was grateful. He didn't talk much, at all. Except to wildly compliment Rachel's cooking.

She'd made roast chicken, potatoes and string beans—Nora's favorite dinner from childhood, which she still seemed to enjoy. She'd also bought a lemon meringue pie at the bakery, which somehow seemed to suit the occasion.

Every once in a while, he'd shoot Rachel a look of longing that turn her insides into a chocolate lava cake.

It was hard for her, too. Harder than he could ever realize. Now they would lose three precious nights together. It didn't seem fair.

When dinner was over, Rachel started clearing the table. Nora got up to help. Jack picked up Charlie out of his high chair.

"I'll give him his bath and get him ready for bed, Rachel. You stay with your sister."

Rachel thanked him, thinking his gesture was considerate. As usual.

Nora watched him as he left the room. She edged closer to Rachel, her voice low. "He even gives Charlie a bath? How long did you say you've been seeing him?"

"Oh...not very long. We've only gone out...a few times."

That part was true. They didn't know each other long and didn't leave the house much. After working hard all day, they spent most of their free time in her bedroom.

"He's very comfortable around here. Very...familiar. Knows where everything is. Acts like he practically lives here."

"Nora." Rachel laughed. "Jack's just the helpful type."

"I can see that. Do you like him?"

Rachel was surprised by Nora's blunt question. "Yes, I like him very much."

"His work is seasonal, I suppose. There aren't many high paying jobs in a place like this. Especially if you don't have an education."

Nora's slight to Jack stung. So he hadn't gone to college. Big deal. He was obviously intelligent. College wasn't for everyone. She'd never been that great a student herself, though she'd always loved art. If she hadn't pursued a degree in design, perhaps she wouldn't have gone to college either.

Nora of course had always been a grind at school and had never really stopped. The walls in her office were covered with certificates of study and all kinds of advanced degrees in her field.

"He enjoys his work. He's very creative. I'll show you what he did in the cottage. It's a real transformation."

Nora didn't seem to hear her.

"A stable income is important Rachel. Especially since you're running a small business. You have to think about your son." Rachel held her tongue. There didn't seem any use trying to convince Nora of Jack's good points.

"I ran into Eric recently. At the opera. He asked me about you," Nora glanced at her.

Rachel was surprised at how little she felt at the mention of her former fiancé. Even a month ago, she would have been jumping in her skin to hear what he'd said and asked and if it seemed he was involved with anyone.

"Really? How is he?" She rinsed off a pot and placed it on the dish drainer.

"He's very well. He still looks great, you have to grant him that." Nora had always liked Eric. Sometimes Rachel thought Nora would have liked to date him herself, though he was somewhat younger. They did have a lot in common, now that she thought about it.

"He asked me about you. He said he wanted to call. I hope you don't mind that I told him where you were living now?"

"No, I don't mind. I was mad at him for a long time. But I'm not any more," she said honestly.

"Oh, well that's good. I think he still has feelings for you, Rachel. I think he has regrets."

Regrets? Well, too late now, Rachel thought.

Nora was quiet for a moment, then she said. "I didn't mention anything about the baby. I wasn't sure you'd want him to know."

"I wouldn't have minded, Nora," Rachel replied evenly.

Nora sounded as if she'd been ashamed to tell Eric about her nephew. But Rachel wasn't surprised. She doubted Eric would ever call her. It was just one of those things people said.

"Does Jack know about Charlie? Where he came from?" she asked in a whisper.

Nora made it sound as if Rachel had ordered her baby on the Internet.

Rachel could have been evasive, but chose to deal with it head on. "No. He doesn't. I haven't told him yet. I have told him I don't have any contact with Charlie's father."

"Oh, is that how you explained it?" Nora shook her head. "Well, maybe you should tell him the truth sometime. It's only fair."

She did have a point. Jack had some secrets. But she had some too.

"I will. If things get serious." Rachel turned to her. "Not everyone thinks like you do, Nora. That it's such a shameful secret."

Nora lifted her chin. "You'd like to believe that, Rachel. I understand. But you're not being realistic. You never were. Open your eyes. The world isn't the rosy picture you want to see. People will…disappoint you. Believe me." Nora nodded and kept rubbing a dinner plate with a dish cloth till it shined.

Rachel knew Nora had been disappointed by her ex-husband. She'd never expected he'd ask for a divorce and she'd never gotten past the hurt.

Rachel had been disappointed by Eric. But somehow, she'd used the painful experience as a spring board to launch herself into a new life.

She suddenly felt sad for her sister, who hadn't discovered that possibility.

Rachel reached out and touched Nora's hand. "Nora, if someone can't accept me and Charlie for who we are, then they don't belong in our life. Plenty of people do accept us. And love us, just the way we are," she said quietly.

She wasn't just talking about Jack and her secret anymore. She was talking about her relationship with Nora.

Nora had reached out her. Made contact. But was she willing to accept her? To live with the fact that there were things they disagreed about and always would, but they were still sisters?

Nora nodded and set the dinner plate down. "I understand what you're saying…I know I've disappointed you. I'm sorry. I guess that's all I came here to say. I do disagree with the choices you've made. But I can see now I shouldn't have just abandoned you. Maybe I thought things wouldn't work out for you, Rachel, and you'd come running to me for help. Like you did when we were little girls. But they have worked out. You've managed to do fine without me."

Rachel was surprised and touched by Nora's apology.

She didn't know what to say. She stepped forward and hugged her sister.

"I still need my big sister. Charlie still needs his aunt. You're all we've got Nora. Mom would have never wanted us to stay angry and out of touch."

Nora nodded. "You're right. Mom always tried to bring us together when we were children, no matter what we'd done to each other."

Rachel could see she was starting to cry. Rachel thought she might cry too.

She squeezed Nora's hand. "I was a little pain some time, wasn't I? I always wanted to be with you and your friends."

"I couldn't get rid of you. A real tag-along. My friends didn't mind. They thought you were cute. I couldn't stand you getting all the attention," she admitted with a smile.

Rachel smiled too but realized it must have been hard for Nora to share, to have a baby sister come along after almost ten years of being an only child. Of course she was jealous at times.

"Remember when I gave your favorite doll a haircut one day while you were at school? You kept her on a very high shelf in your room, but I got at it anyway. You didn't even yell. You were just...sad."

"Yes, I remember." Nora sighed, looking sad at the thought all over again. "I knew you were a baby and didn't know what you were doing."

Rachel nodded. That seemed to the key. Nora would always think of her as the baby, the little sister who needed guidance and advice. Who didn't know what she was doing.

"You don't have to worry about me, Nora. I know what I'm doing. If I make mistakes, they're mine to fix or live with. You know?"

"I can see that now. You've done well up here, Rachel. You should be proud."

Rachel felt stunned. Someone could have just told her

she'd won the lottery. Never in a million years would she have guessed her sister would ever say those words.

She took a breath and met Nora's gaze. "Thank you," she said quietly. "I am proud."

Jack strolled into the room, carrying Charlie high on his broad shoulder. The front of his shirt was splashed with water, but he didn't seem to mind.

"Here he is. Clean as a whistle."

Charlie was dressed in soft, yellow one-piece pajamas. He looked very fresh from his bath and smelled divine, Rachel thought as she snuggled him.

"I have his bottle all ready." She picked up the bottle from the counter top. "Nora, would you like to feed him?"

Nora looked surprised. But nodded quickly. "I'll try."

"Sit right over here," Rachel directed her to a comfortable chair and put Charlie in her lap. Then showed her how to hold him. "Just tilt the bottle a little so he doesn't swallow too much air. He'll do the rest."

"Oh, yes. I can see that. He does seem hungry."

Nora kept her gaze fixed on Charlie, very focused on her job.

"You can talk to him a little," Rachel suggested. "He likes that."

Nora smiled slightly. "Hello, Charlie. I'm your aunt. Aunt Nora. I live in New York. It's not that far," she added.

Rachel slipped back to the kitchen where Jack was waiting for her. He pulled her into a crushing embrace. They shared a long passionate kiss, trying to keep it silent but it was very difficult.

Rachel had visions of making love on the kitchen counter. Impossible with Nora in the next room. But a sweet fantasy.

Finally, Jack loosened his hold, his head dropping to her shoulder a moment as he took a ragged breath. "Okay, one more night. But you'd better clear your calendar for tomorrow, babe. No more house guests."

His threatening tone was thrilling.

"Did you have a good talk with your sister?"

"Yes, we got a lot out in the open. I think it's going to be a lot better now. Maybe she'll come back at Christmas."

It was just a thought. Rachel would have to see if they stayed in touch. But it would be nice to have some family here for Charlie's first Christmas.

Then she realized Jack wouldn't be here anymore.

She wondered if he was thinking the same thing. He seemed suddenly pensive.

"Well, I'd better go. See you tomorrow."

Rachel didn't answer, just watched him leave the kitchen and head downstairs to the back door.

His absence in her life seemed unimaginable. But it would happen. Sooner than she expected.

Chapter Ten

Nora insisted on leaving early the next morning before Rachel opened the shop. They stood outside in the cool mountain air as Nora tossed her overnight bag and huge leather purse into the backseat of her car.

"Saturday must be your busiest day. I don't want to be a bother. I'll be back soon," she promised.

"I hope so. Maybe you could come up for Christmas."

"Maybe I will." Nora nodded, looking pleased at the invitation.

"I'd like to look in some of those little antique shops," she added. "I did find a few small gifts for the office, for my assistant and secretary."

"Really? What did you get?"

She picked up a brown shopping bag and set it down on the floor in the back seat. "Some maple syrup and cheddar cheese. In that cute General Store. It seemed pricey, but it's packed nicely, in little baskets."

Rachel couldn't help but smile, thinking of clever Ella Krueger and her trips to Florida.

Nora leaned over and gave Rachel a quick hug. Then she bent down to Charlie, who sat in his stroller and kissed him on the cheek.

"The next time I see you you'll be running all over the place," she said to her nephew.

Charlie didn't answer. But he did wave.

"Yes, good bye, Charlie," Nora waved at him, then looked back at Rachel briefly as she slipped into the driver's seat.

"Bye now. I'll call you. Oh, and please say good bye to Jack for me? It was…interesting to meet him."

Rachel nodded. "Yes, I will."

Jack had started work very early and they could hear him hammering and sawing in the distance.

She felt sad to see her sister go. But they'd worked through their differences—most of them, anyway—and they were on the right track.

"Drive safely. I'll speak to you soon."

She watched Nora back her car out of the driveway and then disappear down Main Street.

As she walked back up to the house, Jack appeared.

"Was that your sister leaving so early? I wanted to say good-bye."

"That's all right. She knew you were working. She didn't want to interrupt."

"So…does she approve of me? Or does she say I'm not good enough for you?"

Rachel glanced at him. She couldn't tell if he was joking. He almost sounded as if they were in a serious relationship, one with a real future. Which they both knew, was not the case.

"She doesn't approve of you. But she barely approves of me, so I wouldn't worry about it."

She paused and looked up at him, crossing her arms over

her chest. "Did you overhear any of our conversation while you were giving Charlie his bath?"

Jack shrugged. She could tell by the look on his face and the faint shade of red creeping up his tanned cheeks that he had overheard…something.

"No, not really. Not on purpose."

The bathroom wall did share a wall with the kitchen. She should have remembered that.

She didn't know what to say. She met Jack's gaze, then looked away.

"Rachel, I don't think there's anything you could tell me about yourself that would bother me. If that's what you're worried about."

She sighed, her worries melted by the warm, tender light in his eyes. "I feel the same about you." She reached out and touched his arm.

He gazed down at her, his expression suddenly serious. She felt he wanted to say something, but couldn't find the words. Or the courage.

Then he pulled her close and kissed her. She could feel his body, hard and ready to make love.

"You distract me, Rachel," he murmured into her hair. "I'll never get that cottage done."

She only wished that was true.

She eased away from him slowly, feeling a certain feminine power. She gave him a small smile.

"Back to work, then. I have to open the store."

She got behind the stroller and started it pushing it to the house.

"Work…that's all you women ever think about."

He sounded grouchy and frustrated. She could tell he had some idea about going back upstairs to her bed now that Nora was gone.

"That's not fair, Jack. You know that's not true." She turned and started walking back to the house. Then glanced over her shoulder. "By the way, you can move your things back inside when you get a chance."

She could tell from his wolfish grin her meaning was clear.

Jack flipped open a can of paint, stirred it up and carefully poured some into a paint bucket. He dipped in the brush and applied it to the new molding he'd put in around the windows with practiced strokes.

The work was going slowly, so slowly now he was almost moving backward. That would have been funny, if the situation was at all as it appeared.

But it wasn't a simple romance, as Rachel seemed to believe. He was finding it harder and harder to lie to her. And impossible to tell the truth.

Each time he had a chance, he lost his nerve. It never seemed the right moment, the right mood. When he'd first come here, his biggest fear about revealing his identity had been that Rachel would never let him see Charlie again. Now it was far worse. His terror was double. Once he told Rachel how he'd tricked her, he would lose them both.

He'd never felt this way about a woman and it scared him.

Even if he confessed his true feelings, he was sure she'd be so angry, she'd never let him near her again.

On this last trip to New York, he'd met with his lawyer and confided his predicament. He told his attorney everything. Except his true feelings for Rachel. Jack had a feeling the perceptive Mike Heath had guessed. You couldn't rise to the top of his profession without an uncanny sense for reading people.

Mike knew Jack had searched for the mother of his child. But had no idea of the mess he'd made of it.

"What are my rights? I mean, if she fights me."

"Jack, what you've done, however innocent your intentions, it's…indefensible. If you had any rights at all in the situation—which I'm sure you signed away completely when you made the sperm donation—assuming a false identity, insinuating yourself into this woman's life are wrong. No court in the world will have a shred of sympathy for you."

Jack frowned, but didn't answer. He knew the attorney was right.

"If we brought this to trial, you'd be lucky if you weren't charged with…with stalking her, or perpetrating a confidence scheme of some kind."

Jack sank back in the thick leather arm chair. The way his attorney described it made him sound so cold and calculating. So…diabolical.

Getting to know Rachel and Charlie, growing close to them, his irresistible attraction and the magic he felt in her arms…all that was anything but. It was had been the warmest, most honest moments he'd known in his entire life.

He could never explain it to Mike. He doubted he could explain it to anyone.

"Well, at least you're honest with me," he said finally.

"That's what you pay me for, isn't it?" His attorney looked down at a long yellow legal pad, where he'd been making some notes. "This has to be settled out of court. No question. She doesn't have the means to hire a real lawyer. We'll definitely have the advantage. We can put together a nice package for her—child support, college tuition, private grade school. Trips abroad, summer camps…"

"Rachel isn't like that," Jack shook his head. "She won't be bought off."

"You don't know that. Besides, it's not for her, it's for the child. All the things she can't give him growing up, and you can. If she's a good mother, she'll put her own feelings aside. She'll want what's best for her son."

Our son. If only they could raise him together. He loved them both. With all his heart and soul. That should have been the offer. The package he was offering. But she'd never believe him now.

"She is a good mother. They don't come any better," Jack said quietly. "I'll give Charlie everything he needs and more, no matter what. Even if she won't let me see him until his twenty-first birthday."

"Jack, slow down. This is going to be a negotiation. It will probably be better to keep your name out of it. For as long as possible, anyway."

"I know you're just doing your job. But I won't hide behind you. Let her know my identity. I've been dishonest long enough."

"All right. If that's the way you want it." Mike placed the pad on the glossy black conference table, a slim silver pen on top. "What's your time frame on this?"

Jack shifted uncomfortably in his chair.

This was getting too real.

"You mean, for you to contact her?"

"That's right. I can have a draft ready by tomorrow. You review it, send it back with any changes and the final document can be in her hands by Monday morning."

Whoa, that was moving a little too efficiently for him. The minute that letter arrived, his time with Rachel was over.

In fact, if he had any sense at all, he'd be gone before it got there.

He swallowed hard. "That's too fast. I need to finish the work she hired me for. I can't leave her stuck with the place half done. That's the least I can do."

Mike nodded, but didn't say anything. Jack could tell by the expression on the older man's face he understood the unspoken reasons for Jack's delay.

"All right. I suppose you are obligated. You signed a contract with her, didn't you?"

Jack nodded. "I did."

"We don't need you violating that agreement on top of everything else."

"That would be another problem," Jack agreed. He felt

relieved to hear he had a sensible reason to squeeze out more time with her. As well as his private ones.

"How long do you think it will take to finish up?" Mike sat back, balancing the silver pen between his fingertips.

Jack shrugged. He didn't want to be pinned down to a timetable. "I'm not sure. Not too long. I'm mostly done, it's just the finish work."

Mike looked down at his notes. "Let's say a week then. Would that be sufficient?"

"A week? I think so."

Perhaps in a week's time he'd find the courage to confess. To deal with Rachel on his own, before all the legal experts got involved.

As if reading his mind, his lawyer said, "That gives you some time to come clean with her. Bare your soul. She sounds like the sympathetic type. You should use that to your advantage," the attorney advised. "That would probably be the best first step here, Jack. Either way, I think you'll get some rights to see your son. You sound as if there's no limit to what you're willing to do."

"You've got that right. There is absolutely no limit," Jack confirmed. When it came to Charlie, he'd give, say or do anything he had to do.

He'd left the city directly from that meeting and driven up to Vermont, determined to tell Rachel the truth. But when he arrived, there was Nora, and he was banished to the cottage for the night—with the paint cans, power tools and excess stuffed animals.

Now that he had Rachel to himself again, he felt as if he was losing his nerve. He knew why, too. Every time he had the impulse to tell her, he'd look into those big blue eyes, so sweet and trusting. So full of feeling for him. He just couldn't stand the idea of losing that, the way she looked at him. He couldn't stand the idea of all her loving feelings for him turning to anger and disdain.

She already expected him to leave when the job was done. She believed he was not the dependable type, a commitment-shy guy who couldn't settle down. That's the impression she had of him. She accepted it, too.

Wasn't it less hurtful to let her go on believing that, than telling her the truth?

He painted quickly, trying to finish the room before it grew dark. Rachel had already started dinner. He could smell the cooking food wafting from the kitchen window, out across the back yard. Drawing him to her.

He was eager to get inside, to sit at the cozy, warm kitchen with Rachel and Charlie. Eager to end his day with one of their special nights together.

Maybe it would be best to let her learn through a letter. A letter she'd open when he was gone.

Later that night, when dinner was done and Charlie bathed and rocked to sleep, Jack didn't waste a minute leading Rachel to her bedroom and tossing her onto the mattress. Rachel was not surprised; all through dinner that had been her plan, too.

But she was surprised at his passion, the way he made love as if they'd been apart for weeks, instead of days. As if he wanted to lose himself completely in her body.

Yet, he somehow made it last forever, leading her closer and closer to the edge, but never quite letting go. Her pleasure was sharp and tantalizing. The sweetest torture she'd ever known. Finally, she slipped over the peak and lost all control, shattering in Jack's arms like a star, exploding in the heavens.

Jack reached the same terrific height, crashing down in her embrace and calling out her name. They lay still and silent, their limbs entwined. Rachel didn't dare stir. She lay perfectly still, her eyes closed, cherishing the feeling of Jack's body on top of her, as close as two could ever be.

She felt unaccountably sad and knew instinctively that he

did, too. Sad that their time together was coming to an end and there didn't seem to be anything either could do to change that.

Since touring the cottage with Julia the night before Nora came, Rachel had avoided the place. She didn't want to see the daily progress Jack was making. He seemed to be working faster now than ever before. He seemed to have a private deadline that was even sooner than the one they'd agreed upon. She wondered if he'd lined up another job to follow this one and hadn't told her yet.

She wouldn't have been surprised. He liked his secrets.

As she closed the shop on Wednesday, there seemed no avoiding it. Jack stood in the doorway, wearing his paint clothes and holding an official looking clipboard. She remembered the clipboard from the day she'd signed the contract, but hadn't seen it since.

"Rachel, are you closing up now?"

She nodded. "Just about."

"Can you come out to the cottage? I'd like to go over a few things with you."

That sounded ominous, she thought, but she managed to keep a calm expression on her face. "I'll be out in a minute. I'm just finishing the inventory book."

Rachel kept a careful record of every item in her stock, marking off what she sold each day. There was so much in the store, she liked to keep track.

She wished she had some other excuse to put off going over Jack's clipboard list. The request was not a good sign. But he stood just outside the door, patiently waiting for her to finish and she knew there was no putting it off.

Charlie was in his play space, fascinated by his pop-up bar that made more squeaky and ringing sounds than Rachel would have preferred. Rachel picked him up and carried him out with her. Jack smiled at the sight of the baby and Charlie reached out to him.

"Want to take him?" Rachel offered.

Jack seemed about to, then pulled back. "No, I shouldn't. I'm all covered with paint."

Rachel nodded but didn't say anything. Being dirty from work had rarely kept Jack from showing Charlie affection. But she supposed he was trying to be careful of the baby's clothes.

As they walked across the backyard, Rachel remembered the day Jack had come to the shop and the first time they'd walked out here together. It had been only weeks, but felt so long ago.

He opened the front door easily, which had been planed and painted, and the finicky lock was now replaced. He stepped aside politely, allowed her to walk in ahead of him.

The faintly musty smell of the place had been replaced by the odor of fresh paint and varnish. The once stained walls and ceilings were smooth and white. The last of the day's sunlight poured through the new windows and skylights.

Rachel tipped her head back and looked up at the vaulted ceiling—a vast improvement over the old, sagging and stained tile.

"I don't remember talking about a ceiling fan. It's nice, though."

"I found that on sale at the building supply store. Those high ceilings trap the heat. I thought it would be a good idea for you."

"It's a great idea. Did it cost much?"

"Hardly anything at all. I saved on some other items. It won't change the bottom line."

He picked up the clipboard and went down his list for the living room. Ceiling, wall board, windows, refinished floor. Everything seemed in order.

They walked back to the kitchen, now set off from the larger space by a snack bar. "Did you see the new cabinets yet?" he asked. "I think they were a good choice."

"Yes, they are," Rachel agreed. She'd seen a sample but could never picture how these things actually looked for real.

The cabinets were the least expensive kind, he'd told her. But they didn't look it. They did have some style and were most of all, a vast improvement over the ancient set that had been hanging there. A new sink and counter tops made the entire room look clean and up-to-date.

Jack checked more items off the list. The rest went quickly, the short hallway and small bedroom. The bathroom was small, too, and both of them, along with Charlie, couldn't fit inside comfortably. As Jack showed her some special design feature of the new shower stall, she had to step out into the hall.

He was still in the bathroom when Rachel pulled open the next door, which led to the rear bedroom where Jack had slept.

"Oh...that room's not done yet," Jack stepped forward, trying to distract her. But it was too late.

Rachel didn't notice if the repairs in there had been completed or not. Her attention was captured by a state of the art laptop set up on the rickety old night table she'd salvaged for him, and beside that, a BlackBerry.

The bed was most interesting though, covered by huge, nearly transparent sheets of paper filled with complicated diagrams. What looked to Rachel like building plans of some sort.

Rachel couldn't have been more surprised if she'd found another woman lying naked in the bed.

Her mouth hung open as she turned to him. "What's all this? Do you have another job somewhere?"

He took a breath and nodded. The guilty look on his face made her stomach curl. "I do have...something going. Yes."

"So you're in a hurry now to finish here. To have me sign off on everything."

Her voice was flat, emotionless. Merely stating a fact.

"Why didn't you just tell me that straight out? Why do have to keep so many secrets Jack? After all this time, don't you trust me?"

He sighed out loud. His dark gaze fixed on her. "I do trust you, Rachel. You can never know how much."

I trust you with the one thing I treasure the most in the entire world.

"If you really trusted me, Jack, you wouldn't be disappearing all the time without any explanation. You wouldn't be leading some sort of double life."

She saw the blood drain from his face and knew she'd scored a bull's eye. Though she took no satisfaction in that.

"Rachel, I'm sorry. I've made a big mistake coming here. Getting involved with you...and Charlie." He swallowed hard, unable to speak. "I never meant to hurt you. I wish you could believe at least that."

Somehow, deep in her heart, she did believe him. But it was cold comfort to her now.

"It always ends this way for you, doesn't it Jack? I don't think it's me. I bet you can't get close to anyone. Maybe it's the way you were raised, it's hard for you to let anyone close."

He nodded, his expression growing distant and resigned.

"I thought it might be different with you, Rachel. I really did think there was a chance...."

"Don't bother. You don't need to try and make me feel better. I knew what I was getting into. We both knew our...arrangement wasn't going to last forever. Let's not make a big thing out of this. You're obviously ready to move on. That's just fine."

She was trying to sound as if she was handling this perfectly. But she feared she sounded anything but. "How much longer do you need?"

How about a lifetime? he wanted to say. In the mood she was in, he doubted she'd have any interest in that offer.

"I need two more days. Until Saturday. I think that should do it."

"Okay then, that should do it," she echoed sharply. "Do you want me to sign something now?" She looked down at the clipboard, avoiding his gaze.

"No, not yet. When I'm completely finished."

"Okay. Let me know."

Rachel felt as if everything really important between them—their relationship—was finished right now.

She hugged Charlie close and swept past him, down the short hall and straight to the door. Which she nearly slammed behind her.

Jack didn't come upstairs to have dinner that night. She didn't expect him to. But when she heard the sound of his truck peeling out of the driveway, she felt a new wave sadness wash over her.

She sat feeding Charlie. The little boy seemed to sense her unhappiness and reached out to pat her cheek. The gesture made her smile for a moment, the sticky imprint of his hand, comforting.

Rachel didn't feel like eating supper herself. The kitchen seemed empty without Jack. She gave Charlie a quick bath, then went to bed early with a book. She didn't intend to be listening for Jack's return, but she couldn't help herself. The book didn't hold her interest. She didn't think anything could tonight.

She felt so drained and heartbroken, she didn't even feel like talking to Julia. Her friend had gone to San Diego for a few days on business, a Realtor's conference. Rachel didn't want to bother her. She would wait a few days to cry on her pal's shoulder.

Finally, she shut the light and tried to fall asleep. The bed seemed huge and cold. She had known all along what she was getting into, falling for Jack. She'd known from the start the kind of man he was. What he was willing to give. And not give. Why did it still hurt so much? That part didn't seem fair either.

She didn't want to cry over him. He wasn't crying over her right now, she was sure of that. But when she closed her eyes, hot tears spilled out the corners and down her cheeks. She just couldn't help it.

Chapter Eleven

*T*hursday. Friday. Saturday.

The longest three days of her life.

She felt trapped on a forced march across the Sahara. Rachel didn't know how she was going to make it. She'd even considered closing the shop, packing up Charlie and disappearing somewhere until it was over.

Until Jack was gone.

But Friday morning, she started all over again. She dug in, she used every once of her willpower. She wasn't made that way. She wasn't a quitter. She never ran from a fight. She wouldn't lose all that business either, just because of him. That would make her even madder.

She had hired Julia's mother, Lucy, to come in on the weekends. With someone in the shop it would also give her a chance to sneak off for a few hours if she had too.

Thursday and Friday went by without a single sighting of Jack, though she knew for sure by the furious sound of his hammer and power drill late into the night, he was in there.

Her own feelings went up and down like a roller coaster, from shocked, to heartbroken, to insanely angry.

Saturday morning, she woke up exhausted and could hardly drag herself out of bed. She pulled her hair back into a low ponytail and pulled on the first thing she saw in the closet, just to start the day.

She went into the shop early and occupied herself re-folding every folded garment on the shelves and tables. When would Jack go? This morning? This afternoon? At the end of the day? She had no idea now of his progress, how much he'd done and what was left to do. She wondered if he would say good-bye face-to-face, or somehow manage to slip away, leaving her a note or something.

She was glad to see Lucy Martinelli walk in at ten, even though she was late. Lucy didn't have a great sense of time, but Rachel wasn't a stickler for things like that.

"Good morning," Lucy greeted her gaily. "My, you look tired, dear. Did the baby keep you up? I hope he's not sick again."

"Charlie's fine. I've just had some trouble sleeping lately."

"You're working too hard. Just like Julia. You young women, so ambitious and independent. I admire that." Lucy nodded at her.

Rachel forced a small smile. She and Julia, two of a kind. The way things were going, they would end up alone, without anyone. At least they'd have each other.

"When is Julia coming back from California? I know she told me, but I forgot."

"She should be back Sunday night. Or is it Sunday morning? I'm not sure how it works out with the time change." Lucy shook her head. "I hope she's having a good time. Meeting people." Rachel knew that was Lucy's code word for "men." "She can use a little more fun in her life. She doesn't take after me that way," Lucy said innocently. "But her father was always the serious type."

"Julia's mentioned that," Rachel replied. Julia had told her own version of her parents' marriage, a match of total opposites. Rachel was sure it was very different from Lucy's memories.

"I can't believe September is almost over. Didn't the month go by quickly?"

Lucy had no idea. The days had been a fast forward blur since she'd met Jack.

"I think as you get older, time seems to pass faster and faster." Lucy glanced at Rachel and nodded. "Remember to grab it with both hands, Rachel, and enjoy what you can."

Rachel swallowed a lump that had suddenly formed in her throat. "I try, Lucy. I do try."

Lucy's advice was true but in some ways hard to follow. Rachel had thought she was doing the "life with both hands thing," having an affair with Jack. But right now she wished she'd never let herself get involved with him.

Time did seem to go quickly when you were happy and life was good. But when you were sad and secretly suffering, a day or even an hour could seem endless. Her few weeks with Jack had passed in the blink of an eye and now she looked at a long, bleak winter.

A customer strolled in, a pretty young woman who was pregnant. Normally Rachel enjoyed waiting on the expectant mothers, but this time she let Lucy field it.

She carried Charlie into his nursery and set him down for his morning nap. She cuddled him close, rocking him to sleep, breathing in his warm, wonderful baby smell. She had this nap business down pat by now. She knew just the way to hold him, the walking and rocking pace, the tune to hum.

According to the child care books, he'd soon be past the

stage of needing two naps a day. He'd go down to one in the afternoon. Then none. It seemed as if every time she mastered a stage with him, he had just about outgrown it.

Once Charlie was in the Portacrib, she sat down in a nearby chair. She heard Lucy out in the shop, taking care of the customer. She decided to stay with Charlie and wait until he'd fallen asleep.

She heard the door on the shop door ring and then heard a man's voice, speaking to Lucy. She thought it must be Jack and was glad she was hidden from view.

A moment later, Lucy appeared at the nursery door. "Sorry to bother you, Rachel. There's a man here to see you. I told him you were busy. But he said that he'd wait."

A man there to see her. She couldn't imagine who that could be. She didn't owe anyone money, thank goodness. Could it be someone looking for Jack? Something to do with his mysterious trips?

Rachel hoped not. She took a breath and smoothed down her long skirt. If Jack really was in trouble, she realized, no matter what she'd said, she knew she would defend him. Help him, any way she could.

She stepped out of the back room and looked around. A tall man stood near the counter, his back turned to her. He had blond hair and broad shoulders. He wore a chocolate brown suede jacket and khaki pants.

She felt her mouth go dry.

It couldn't be possible.

But when he turned and smiled at her, she knew she hadn't been imagining it.

"Rachel...sorry to surprise you like this. But I wasn't sure you'd speak to me if I called."

Eric Rowland stepped towards her, a humble smile on his handsome face. Rachel's head popped up as she looked at him, like a little bobble head doll on the back of someone's dashboard.

"Eric...how did you find me?" *Why* did you find me, was more the question she'd like him to answer.

"I ran into your sister. At Lincoln Center. She told me she hadn't seen you in a while, but she planned to come up here."

"She did visit, just last week. She told me you might call," Rachel replied. *Not surprise me on one of the worst days of my life.*

"I didn't even know you'd left the city."

There was a lot about her he didn't know anymore.

"I left a few months ago. I wanted to start my own business. Someplace less crowded."

"You certainly found that." Eric chuckled.

Eric had never liked the country. Even for a weekend. She remembered one time when they went to Block Island for a romantic weekend and he'd had a fit because he couldn't find the Sunday *New York Times*. When they were engaged, it was clear that even if they'd had children, Eric would never move out of the city.

"It's a beautiful old building," he said. "And a very pretty store. You always were creative. What gave you the idea for a place like this?"

Rachel shrugged. "I always enjoyed designing children's wear," she reminded him. "And I had a baby."

Rachel took some guilty pleasure in shocking him. But he quickly recovered. Eric was always good at that.

"A baby. Wow. A boy or a girl?"

"A boy. His name is Charlie."

He nodded. "How nice. That's great news."

Then there was a dead silence. She knew that he was wondering now if she was married. She caught him checking her hands for rings.

She decided to let him dangle.

"So...is there a husband or partner or something, whose going to run in here and wonder why you're talking to your former boyfriend?"

"You can relax. No husband or partner." Or anything at all now, she added silently. "I'm doing this all on my own."

Eric looked surprised again. She guessed he didn't think she had the courage to make that choice. It felt good to show him that she did.

"Good for you, Rachel. Good for you." He nodded, a certain light of respect in his eyes she'd never seen before. "Where is he? Can I see him?"

She'd never recalled Eric having much interest in children. When he spoke about being a parent, it was always in some far off time. After they'd done everything fun they could possibly do as a couple.

But perhaps he'd had a change of heart about babies. He did seem interested now.

"He's having a nap. But you can come back and take a peek."

Rachel was happy to show Charlie off to her former almost husband.

She led him back to the nursery and quietly opened the door. Charlie was still sound asleep, curled on his side under a light blanket. He looked so sweet, nestled against his white dog, his thumb stuck in his mouth.

Eric actually sighed. Rachel had to look at him to make sure he wasn't faking it. But his response seemed genuine.

See what you missed, not marrying me? she wanted to say to him.

"He's beautiful, Rachel. Absolutely...perfect." He gazed at her with admiration. "You're very lucky."

"Thanks. I think I am," she admitted.

She heard the bell on the shop door ring and then heard Jack's voice, talking to Lucy. Lucy quickly appeared at the nursery.

"Jack's here. He says someone's blocking his truck."

Eric looked flustered. "Oh, that must be me. I'd better get out there."

Rachel walked out into the shop and Eric followed her, patting his pockets for his car keys.

Jack stood at the counter, his expression curdling as he realized Rachel had been in a back room of the shop with a man. And one he didn't know.

Eric smiled at Jack, oblivious of the implications. "Sorry I was in your way. I'll move my car right away."

Jack didn't answer, just stared at him.

Rachel touched Eric's sleeve. "Eric, this is Jack Sawyer. He's doing some renovations on the cottage out back." She turned to Jack. "Jack, this is an old friend of mine, Eric Rowland."

"Nice to meet you, Jack." Eric politely offered his hand.

Rachel saw a light bulb go off over Jack's head. He shook Eric's hand, but didn't say anything.

"Sorry, but I have to get over to the lumber yard," Jack said finally.

"Oh, right. Be right back, Rachel," Eric called over his shoulder as he left the store.

Jack didn't move a muscle. He didn't seem to be in such a great hurry, Rachel thought.

"So that's the amazing Eric...and you got mad at me for letting my projects overlap."

Rachel felt the blood rush to her head, like a volcano about to explode. "How dare you say such a thing to me." Her voice was hushed but full of emotion. "I had no idea he was coming here today. This is mainly my sister's doing."

She couldn't tell whether Jack believed her or not. And why should she care?

"Sure, if you say so. Quite a coincidence, though."

"Yes...quite. Don't you need to get over the lumber yard?" she reminded him. "You're supposed to be done out there by tomorrow. Having some delay?"

He stared at her, looking frustrated and unhappy. "Don't worry. I'll be done and out here. Out of your way, so you can play catch-up with your old fiancé."

Rachel felt a pang at his angry response. But she had to admit, she had goaded him into it.

She had no plans to play catch-up or play anything else with Eric. But she didn't have to tell Jack that. It was none of his business.

Eric walked in, wearing a sunny smile. Jack stomped out, nearly knocking him over as the two men passed each other in the narrow aisle.

Rachel had a split second to compare them side by side. Both were tall and fit, though Eric was lankier and Jack more muscular. Eric was fair, with dark blond hair and light eyes. Something about his manner and expression suggested he didn't have a care in the world. A trait that had attracted her at first.

Jack was just the opposite. His hair and eyes were dark, his manner thoughtful, even pensive. While Eric was sunny and often superficial, Jack was brooding and deep.

Rachel found it quite amazing that despite her long relationship with Eric, she felt no spark of attraction for him any longer and despite the painful parting from Jack, her heart still ached with love for him.

Eric walked up to her and smiled. "Do you take a break for lunch at all?"

Rachel felt flustered. She wasn't sure she wanted to spend time with him and didn't know what to say. "Saturdays are sort of wild around here. It's hard to leave."

"Sure, I understand. How about dinner? You don't keep a baby store open all night...do you?"

She had to laugh at his maneuver. "No, I don't stay open all night. I'd need to find a sitter, though."

Lucy had gone back to the nursery and now emerged with Charlie in her arms. "Look who's up," she announced gaily. She picked up Charlie's hand and made him wave. "Wave to Mama, honey."

Eric turned and gave Rachel a look. "Yes, Lucy might babysit," Rachel said. "I'll ask her."

Rachel walked over and took Charlie. Then she asked Lucy if she was free to watch the baby that evening.

"I have no plans. I'd be happy to watch this dumpling boy." Her answer left Rachel no convenient out.

As Rachel walked back to Eric, to tell him the date was on, she realized that maybe some part of her did want to go out with him, just this once. There were some loose ends that needed tying up and questions to resolve.

And attention from the man who had once rejected her did feel good. The balm to her ego *almost* took her mind off of Jack.

When Eric came at seven to pick her up, Jack was still working. The cottage was lit brilliantly with special lights he'd bought for painting and Rachel could see him through the curtainless windows, laying flat on a scaffold as he worked on the high ceiling.

She wondered if he had noticed her leaving with Eric. Probably not, she thought. Which made her wonder why she had agreed to go out with Eric at all.

"I didn't really know where to take you," Eric said, as he drove down Main Street. "I booked a room at an inn in town and everyone recommends the restaurant there."

"The Lion's Head Inn?" Rachel asked.

"That's right. But I bet you've eaten there often. That was dumb of me, right?"

"No, not at all. I've only been there once." With Jack. The night he saved her from the rain storm. "The food is very good," she added. "New York quality...practically."

She didn't want to overpraise the place. Though she did think highly of the cuisine and service. Eric was very fussy about such things. He took dining out very seriously. His standards had always been higher than her own.

"If the food is up to the atmosphere, we'll be fine."

They were right on time for their reservation and seated quickly. Not the same table she'd sat at with Jack, but near enough to make her remember more than she wanted to about her last visit there.

Eric took a long time reviewing the wine list, which gave Rachel too much time for her thoughts to wander.

Jack would be leaving tomorrow. She wondered if he would even say goodbye. But of course, he had to speak to her. She had to sign off on their contract. She wished he could just slip it under the door, or leave it in her mailbox. She wasn't sure she could handle saying goodbye to him, even at their angry distance.

"Rachel? Did you hear me?"

"Oh…I'm sorry. I was just thinking about something."

Eric smiled. "That's all right. You're a businesswoman now, you probably have a lot on your mind. But tonight you can just kick back and relax for a few hours. Just put all those worries on the back burner for a while."

She nodded and smiled. "I'd love to."

They ordered dinner and their waiter brought the wine Eric had chosen.

"This reminds me of the good old days," Eric glanced over at her. "How about a toast?" Before Rachel could answer, he lifted his glass.

"To Rachel, a woman who knows what she wants in life and knows how to make it happen."

Rachel was surprised by his effusive compliment. She touched her glass to his and sipped the wine. "Thank you, Eric. That was quite a compliment. All I really did was go on with my life after our relationship ended."

Eric nodded. "Of course you did. But with great style."

He smiled at her and she had to smile back. "I feel as if I'm meeting you for the first time."

"Well…maybe I deferred to much to you sometimes, when it came to deciding how we would spend our time, or where we would live once we married. Maybe I felt…overpowered by you," she admitted.

"Seems you've found your power now. Are you happy, Rachel?"

"Yes, I am." She nodded, feeling a twinge in her heart about Jack. She forced the thought out of her mind. "Mostly. No one is totally happy," she added. "Life just isn't like that."

"It must be hard to raise a child and run a new business all on your own. Don't you get lonely?"

"Sometimes," she admitted. "But I'm not interested in dating right now," she added quickly. "How about you? Are you seeing anyone?"

"No." He shook his head and looked away for a moment. She sensed there had been someone. Maybe even while they were still engaged. "I did get out there for awhile, right after we broke up. But I haven't met anyone special. No one like you," he added. "I'm just starting to realize what I gave up. I don't know what I was thinking, Rachel."

She knew they would get to this conversation sooner or later. And here they were. After years of imagining what she would say to him if she ever got the chance, Rachel was at a complete loss.

"I don't know what you were thinking either, Eric," she said finally. She sighed.

"Can you ever forgive me for what I did? It was…really awful."

"I was shocked and hurt," she admitted. "But it would have been worse to marry you if you really didn't want to go through with it. You can't marry someone because you don't want to hurt their feelings."

He smiled slightly, looking relieved at her response. He reached over and touched her hand. "You always were a sympathetic soul, Rachel. I never really appreciated that about you."

There was a lot he didn't appreciate about her. But no use making a list now.

The entrees arrived and they ate for a while in silence.

"That guy Jack Sawyer. The guy with the truck. Are you seeing him or something?"

She looked up. "Why do you ask?"

"Oh, I don't know. Just the way he looked at me maybe when you introduced us. Then he nearly ran me over when he finally pulled out. That seemed to be a clue."

Rachel chose her words carefully. "There was something between us. But it wasn't serious. He's leaving tomorrow. Now that the work is done. I don't expect to hear from him again."

It was hard to say the words out loud. As soon as she did, Rachel felt a tight band squeeze her heart. She put her fork aside, suddenly losing her appetite.

"How's your dinner?" Eric looked at her curiously. "Anything wrong?"

"It's delicious. I'm just not as hungry as I thought."

Eric started eating again. "I'm not surprised to hear things didn't go too far. He doesn't seem at all your type."

Rachel didn't answer. Eric had no idea what her type was anymore. But she didn't bother to argue with him.

Rachel changed the subject, asking Eric questions about his work. He was a lawyer at a large firm that had a varied practice. Eric was a trial attorney and very persuasive in court. He was proud that he'd become a partner in his early thirties. Rachel had been impressed by his profession and achievements when they'd first met but didn't quite feel the same now.

"So, how is your work going, Eric?" she asked, turning the conversation away from her private life. "Have you been involved in any big trials lately?"

"As a matter of fact, I have. Maybe you heard about it on the news?" Eric launched into a description of the lawsuit he'd tried in court, representing a famous talk show host in a high profile divorce. Rachel's thoughts wandered. She remembered a lot of these conversations with Eric, when she couldn't quite keep her focus on his long, sometimes tedious stories about legal maneuvering. She saw now that she had narrowly missed a lifetime of such tales.

Eric drove her home and walked her to the back door of the house, the entrance that led to her apartment. "I'm glad we had this time together, Rachel. I know you didn't have to see me…after everything I put you through."

"For a long time I didn't want to see you, Eric," she said honestly. "But now I'm glad I did. It helped me to put things in perspective. It was probably a good thing that we didn't go through with our wedding plans."

"Oh…I'm not so sure about that, Rachel." He gazed down at her, his expression looking sad and thoughtful. "I am for the way I ended things. I think I just got cold feet and didn't know what to do. I don't think I ever really stopped loving you."

Rachel looked up at him, stunned.

Even a month ago, she would have been thrilled to hear Eric say those words and despite everything, willing to try again with him.

It was definitely gratifying to see the man who had broken her heart trying to win her back. But she just didn't feel the same. He'd said it himself, she was a different person in many ways. She saw him differently now too.

And her heart belonged to someone else. The guy with the truck, who Eric thought was so wrong for her. Never mind that Jack didn't seem to want it.

She swallowed hard, not knowing what to say. He clearly expected her to say something. She reached out and touched his arm. "Eric…I'm sorry. I just don't feel the same anymore."

"I hurt you. I hurt you badly. I know you can't just flip a switch and turn things back to the way they were. But do you think that there's any hope at all?"

Rachel sighed and looked up into his searching gaze. "I'm sorry. Everything has changed for me."

He nodded. "I understand. This was probably all too much.

Coming up here and pouring out my heart to you. But I just had to take a chance." He smiled wistfully. "Can we just stay in touch? Can we stay friends? We always were good friends, Rachel."

Rachel felt that way too. You could never have too many friends, her mother used to say. "Sure." She nodded. "That would be a good thing. I'd like to stay in touch with you, Eric."

He smiled tenderly and pulled her close for a moment, then gently kissed her cheek. "Take care of yourself, Rachel," he whispered. "And that little boy, too."

"I will, Eric. Good night." Rachel turned the key in the lock and left him on the door step. When she got upstairs, Lucy was sitting in the kitchen, having a cup of tea.

"Rachel, you surprised me. I thought you'd be back later. Did you have a nice time?"

Rachel slipped off her coat and hung it on a the back of the chair. "It was…interesting."

Lucy met her gaze. "That fellow seemed nice. But a bit…slick. Or maybe it was just—you know—that New York way he has about him."

Rachel smiled. Lucy was a good judge of character. "We were engaged once. He was a bit slick, slipped right out of our wedding plans. I think he just wanted me to know he was sorry."

Lucy nodded. "Well, that was the decent thing to do. I guess he's not so bad after all."

"Yes, maybe," Rachel replied. She didn't know what to think about Eric now. He'd certainly surprised her.

Lucy soon left and Rachel stepped into Charlie's room to check on him. He was sleeping soundly, his cherubic face bathed in the soft golden glow of a nightlight.

If I'd married Eric, I wouldn't have you, she told him silently. *That's another reason I have to thank him for jilting me.*

She left Charlie and started to pick up around the apart-

ment. His toys and baby paraphernalia seemed to be everywhere. She hated to get up in the morning and step over
things.

A knock sounded on the door downstairs. She thought it
was Lucy, who had forgotten her reading glasses. They were
sitting on the kitchen table next to a magazine.

"Come up, Lucy. It's not locked."

The door opened. "It's not Lucy. It's me, Jack."

"Oh…Jack." She went to the top of the stairs and looked
down at him. Her heart pounded so hard against her ribs it
hurt.

"It's sort of late. I was just going to bed," she called down
to him. Then sighed at her choice of words.

"It won't take long. I just want to talk to you for a minute."
His hand was on the railing, his foot on the top step, but he
didn't move forward, waiting for her permission.

"I'm leaving very early tomorrow morning. Everything's
done."

She sighed. This was it. She stepped back from the stair-
case and took a breath.

"Okay. In that case, I guess we had better talk."

Rachel walked back to the kitchen, her thumping heartbeat
matching the sound of Jack's heavy steps on the stairs.

Then he stood in the doorway, staring at her. Dressed in a
leather jacket, black T-shirt and jeans, he looked about as good
as she'd ever seen him. She had the crazy impulse to go to him,
to throw herself in his arms and bury her face against his chest.

Why did this have to happen to her? Why did she let
herself fall in love with him? A man with no known zip code
and a broken down truckload of emotional issues? Not to
mention whatever he'd been hiding from her, a prison record
or something equally as hard to accept.

Jack's expression was grim, his complexion ashen. He
pulled his gaze from hers and tossed a folder on the table. He

flipped it open to reveal the contract they had signed for the renovation.

"Here you are. Just sign it the bottom of that last page and we're all...done."

Rachel stepped over to the table and looked down at their agreement. She took the pen he'd left for her and scribbled her name, as quickly as she could.

Then she stood up and looked at him. "Wait, what about the money I owe you? Don't you need a check?"

Jack scooped up the contract. "That's okay. I haven't figured out the final figure yet. It's going to be less than the estimate. I'll call you and you can send it to me."

Rachel stood back, her arms crossed over her chest. "Is this how you treat all your clients, Jack? I can't see how you can make a living if you don't collect your fee."

He glanced at her, looking uncomfortable. "I...I don't need the money, Rachel. I'm fine. I'll send you a bill. It's not a problem for me."

"All right. I guess that's it, then."

She felt herself getting teary eyed, looking at him and had to turn away. She wished he would just go, before she started crying. She didn't want him to see how much his indifference hurt her.

"Can I say goodbye to Charlie?" he asked quietly.

She was surprised at his request. Then not surprised at all. She knew Jack cared for her son. He'd never held back showing her that.

"He's sleeping. But I guess you can go in and see him."

Jack followed her into the nursery. She let him step close to the crib, while she lingered in the doorway. The expression on his face as he looked down at the sleeping baby, then gently leaned over and kissed Charlie's head...

If love and tenderness counted for anything, Jack would have been a good father to her son. He would have been a great father.

But that was not meant to be either. Finally he turned and took a deep breath. He whisked the back of his hand under his eyes and she thought she he might be crying but couldn't tell in the darkened room.

She walked back into the hallway and he followed. He turned to her, looking as if he had something important to say.

Would he try to kiss her goodbye too? She knew if he touched her, her self control would melt in an instant.

"I know you don't think it's any of my business, Rachel," he began, "but I hope you aren't getting involved with that guy Eric again."

Of all the things she expected him to say at that moment, this was not one on the list.

She stepped back, feeling annoyed at his presumption.

"You're right. It isn't any of your business, Jack."

"Rachel, he's dull and prosaic and full of himself. I don't know how he ever hooked you the first time. You were lucky to get away. He doesn't appreciate you and he'd never be a good father to Charlie."

That last part pushed her over the edge.

She was angry enough at him for coming up here and dragging out this farewell scene. Didn't he see he was breaking her heart even more every second he was near?

Now she had to hear him tell her how to live her life… when he'd made it clear he didn't want any part of it.

"Oh, and you appreciate me, I suppose?" she challenged him. "What right do you have to tell me who would be a good father for Charlie?"

Jack was standing so close to her now she could feel his heat. He stared down, his eyes black.

Suddenly he took her shoulders in his strong grip and practically shook her, quickly cutting off her tirade.

"For heaven's sake, Rachel. I *am* his father," he shouted back.

Rachel reeled back, stunned and speechless. She probably

would have fallen if he hadn't still held on to her. Finally, she shrugged free of his hold.

"What in the world are you trying to say?" she demanded.

"I'm telling you the truth. I know how you got pregnant, Rachel. I know the whole story. Dynamics, Inc. The catalogue. Donor number 35723. Caucasian male. Irish and Swedish decent. Ivy league graduate. Degrees in engineering and architecture…"

"Wait, wait…you can't be serious?" Rachel stared at him in disbelief. How did he know all this? There must be some logical explanation for it…other than the one he'd just announced.

"You can't be Charlie's natural father," she insisted. "It's just…impossible. I don't know what kind of game you're trying to play here, Jack."

"This is not a game, Rachel," he said, cutting her off. He stared at her and took a deep breath. "I've tried to tell you the truth. I could just never get it out. This isn't the way I wanted you to find out either. I came here with the best intentions. I just wanted to see Charlie. And find out if you were a good mother."

Rachel's gaze narrowed. "You came here to spy on us, you mean? Those were your good intentions?"

Jack shook his head. "I found out I was a father, Rachel. It was quite a shock. I had to make sure the mother of my child was a decent, responsible person…."

"And after you found out that part, you had to trick me into hiring you to fix the cottage, into trusting you, making love with you…"

"Rachel, please, it wasn't like that. I didn't mean for any of that to happen. And then the more I got to know you, the harder it was for me to tell you the truth."

Rachel could barely take it all in. Jack was not…Jack. He really did have a double life. He really did have a secret. Nothing she would have imagined in a thousand years.

"So who the hell are you? Is Jack Sawyer even your real name?"

"Of course it is, I didn't lie about that. Here, want to see my license?" He made a move to take out his wallet, but Rachel shook her head.

"Save it. Identification can be fake, even I know that. I suppose that sad story about being abandoned by your mother isn't true either, is it?"

"Every thing I told you about my past was true, Rachel. I just left out a few things about my present. I'm not some local handyman. I'm an architect. I'm good at what I do. I have a firm in Manhattan." He paused and met her gaze again. "I can give our son everything, Rachel. I can help you, too. I want to help you." For a split second, his soft, sincere tone was nearly Rachel's undoing.

"So you're rich. So what? You're not going to take Charlie away from me. No matter how much money you have. You're not going to buy back your own son."

"That's not what I meant at all. I just want to be part of his life. I love Charlie, too." He moved toward her, looking dark and powerful, his voice tight with emotion. "I'd fight you for that much, Rachel. If I have to."

Rachel held her ground. She stared up at him, her expression fierce, her blue eyes flashing.

"Get out of here. Get out right now, before I call the police. You don't have any rights around here yet," she reminded him.

Jack stared at her a moment, his face without expression. Then he turned and walked down the stairs. She leaned on the stair railing, feeling herself shaken to the core, suddenly unable to stand without support.

Seconds later, she heard the door downstairs slam shut and Jack's truck roar down the driveway.

Rachel collapsed to the floor and covered her face with hands, her body rocked by powerful sobs.

Jack was not Jack. He was someone else entirely.

She'd fallen in love with a phantom. An illusion. A man who didn't even exist. And now the actor had pulled off his mask. And he was her worst nightmare.

A darkly handsome thief who had come to steal her son.

Rachel sat alone on the floor in the dark hallway, her heartbreak giving way to a wave of ice-cold fear.

Chapter Twelve

The letter arrived from Jack's lawyer early on Monday morning. Holding Charlie in her arms, Rachel stepped out to the porch and signed for it. She stared down at the thick envelope, the expensive vellum stationery and ominous return address.

She knew instinctively it was trouble. A Pandora's Box, once she opened it.

She carried it inside at arm's length, as if it was about to explode. Luckily Julia was there. She'd cut her trip to California short to offer her friend moral support.

"It's not even noon and I've got a letter from his lawyer." Rachel set the letter down on the table where she and Julia sat drinking coffee and strategizing.

Julia had looked Jack up on the Internet and printed out pages of information. He was all he claimed to be, a successful, well-known architect, award-winning and fabulously wealthy.

The photos made Rachel misty eyed again. The articles

proved he was out of her league. She could only imagine the type of women the real Jack Sawyer got involved with. He must have thought she was so quaint and naive. So gullible. The way she'd just jumped into bed with him...

He'd made such a fool of her, she could never forgive him.

Julia picked the letter up. "Don't you even want to see what it says?"

Rachel could already guess what it said. Her stomach hurt too much to actually read it. She held Charlie on her lap while he played with a plastic toy. The last few days, she'd found it hard to let him out of her sight.

"You open it. Please?"

Julia glanced at her. "Okay. If you really want me to."

Julia slipped her finger under the edge of the envelope and tore it open. There were several pages of single-spaced type. Rachel couldn't bear to look any closer than that.

Julia looked it over quickly, her lips moving as she performed a silent speed read.

"He doesn't want to go to court. Wants to settle this 'in a reasonable and amicable way, beneficial for all parties,'" she read. "But he does want joint custody of Charlie. That is serious."

Joint custody? Rachel felt as if an arrow pierced her heart.

"He can't ask for that. He signed away all his parental rights at the clinic. I saw the form with my own eyes."

"It explains about that too. Says he'd been misdiagnosed with a terminal illness at the time and was under great stress, so he wasn't thinking clearly."

Even now, Rachel felt a jolt hearing that Jack had faced that crisis. Thank goodness it had been a wrong diagnosis.

Julia looked up at her. "I guess he's trying to play on your sympathy and also show that's what he'd argue in court."

"It might work. You never know..." She sighed. "What else does it say? All those pages... It looks like a contract."

Julia flipped through the sheaf of pages. "It's a custody

agreement. It basically says you and Charlie will be treated like royalty for the rest of your life, if you give Jack what he wants. He wants to be Charlie's father. He claims he already is."

"I told him he couldn't buy back his child from me. I meant every word of it."

Julia put the document down and looked across the table. She reached out and touched Rachel's hand.

"You ought to look this over for yourself. Sometime when you're feeling calmer and can really think about the consequences. For Charlie. His future. I'm not talking about the material things. Jack wants to be there for him. He does love him...."

Rachel felt stung. Was her best friend turning on her, too?

"You sound as if you're on his side. Don't you understand what it would mean if I signed something like that? Why...Jack would be a part of our life. I'd have to see him all the time."

Julia didn't say anything. Rachel could tell what she was thinking, though. *Would that be such a bad thing? I know you love him.*

Rachel shook her head. "No, I can't. Not after the way he...tricked me and used me. How can I ever trust him again? Or forgive him?"

She really did love him. Julia knew that, too. But she felt so foolish and betrayed.

"Jack has real feelings for you, Rachel. He may not be able to handle them. That's why he could never tell you the truth. I think the way he tricked you was terrible. But he knew once you found out he was Charlie's father, he'd have to go. And he didn't want to leave you, or Charlie."

Julia's words were comforting. But they didn't solve Rachel's dilemma. She didn't want to grant Jack joint custody or anything close to it. She wanted him to disappear where ever he'd come from and leave her and Charlie alone.

"I need a lawyer. I need to fight him. He can't get away

with this. I don't care how much money he has…or if he's willing to make Charlie president."

Julia sighed. "All right. I guess that's a good idea. I can ask around for you. But I don't think any of the lawyers I know around here can handle this situation. Jack's hired some pretty heavy talent."

Rachel could see that. She sat back in her chair. Even if she knew a sharp, New York attorney, she couldn't afford the bills. Jack had probably guessed that though and thought he had her cornered.

Did he?

Charlie tugged on a strand of hair but she barely felt it. Someone knocked on the shop door, then walked in. A deliveryman carrying flowers.

"Flowers for Ms. Rachel Reilly?" he read off a card.

"That's me." Rachel handed Charlie over to Julia. "First a threat from his lawyer, now flowers. He pulls all the stops, doesn't he? As if a bunch of flowers are going to change my mind," she said angrily.

The deliveryman handed over the arrangement. Rachel signed and gave him a tip. She set the vase on the counter and pushed back the tissue paper wrapping to reveal a large expensive bouquet. A mix of roses, hydrangea, lilies—large and small—and other beautiful blossoms she couldn't identify, but were no less lovely.

"Wow, what do you ask for when you get that bouquet? Just send everything you've got?" Julia laughed.

Rachel didn't think it was so funny, but before she could reply she read the card.

"It's not even from Jack. It's from Eric."

"Eric Rowland? Oh, right. I nearly forgot about him," Julia admitted. "For a single mom stuck in the country, you sure lead a busy life. What does he have say?"

"Great to see you again. At least it's a start? More than your friend—Love, Eric."

"Whoa…sounds like he has hopes of getting back together."

Rachel had to agree. "I was very clear with him. But I did agree I'd still be friends. I didn't think he'd take it so seriously."

"He's a lawyer, right? Maybe he can help you, or at least put you in touch with a colleague. Jack obviously has the best money can buy. If you plan on fighting him, you're going to need some help, Rachel."

Rachel knew she was right. She had qualms about turning to Eric, but he seemed to be her best option at the moment. At least he could give her some free advice.

"You're right. I'm going to call him. I have a perfect excuse, thanking him for flowers."

Rachel set the card aside and took Charlie back from Julia. She hugged him close and stroked his hair with her hand.

"This will cost a fortune. I may have to sell the building… but I'll do whatever I have to."

Julia rose from her chair and gave Rachel a hug. "One step at a time, Rachel. I'll help you any way I can. I have money to lend you. Let's not panic."

She tilted her head and caught Julia's eye. "Listen, there is one good thing about Jack leaving. I can finally rent the cottage. That will definitely help you right now. Let me work on that today."

Rachel nodded, thankful for Julia's help. "Okay, thanks. That will help. I'll give you the key. It's all yours."

She took out her key ring and pulled off the one for the cottage front door.

The cottage looked beautiful now, inside and out. Thanks to Jack. Though it was painful for Rachel to go inside there anymore.

Julia soon left for her office, promising to call Rachel later in the day. Rachel gave Charlie a bottle and put him down for a nap. Luckily Mondays were always slow. She wasn't up to handling a rush of customers and had plenty to do.

She called Eric's office and was put through right away.

"Rachel, did you get my flowers already?"

"Yes, I did. You didn't have to that, Eric. But they're very beautiful. They've definitely been a bright spot in the day," she admitted.

"Oh…is something wrong? Nothing wrong with the baby, I hope?"

"Charlie's fine, but I am having a problem. A serious problem. I wondered if you could give me some advice."

"I'd be happy to help you any way I can, Rachel. You know that. What's going on?"

"It's sort of a long story," she warned him.

"I have time. Just tell me. What's the problem?"

Rachel did her best to summarize. She told Eric the whole situation, starting from her decision to become a single mother. She told how Jack had tricked her, hiding his identity and even about their romantic involvement.

Eric didn't say much, mostly listened. He seemed sympathetic and even angry on her behalf.

When she was done, he let out a long sigh. "Rachel, this man has behaved in the most reprehensible manner possible. Even if he does have good lawyers, like you say, he still doesn't have a case. He signed away his rights to the child and he assumed a fake identity to gain your trust. He says he wants to settle this amicably, but that's because he won't dare take this into court. He knows he doesn't have a chance."

Eric's confident manner and legal expertise gave her hope.

"Really? So you think I have chance to keep Charlie?"

"Of course you do. Please, let me help you. I know I can make this go away. And I feel I owe it to you."

"Eric, you don't owe me anything. I didn't call you to collect on some favor."

"I know that. But I feel…responsible. I mean, if I hadn't broken off our engagement, you would have never made the choices that you did. You would have never gone to a sperm bank to have a child, that's for sure."

Rachel couldn't argue with him about that. But she did feel annoyed he'd painted her life choices as a crazy reaction to his rejection. It wasn't that way at all. Not from her perspective.

"Getting left at the altar was tough, Eric. No question. But it gave me the courage to change my life. To give up on the childish idea that you—or any man—was going to complete me. Or give me things I wanted. I love the life I've made. I don't think it was just some impulsive reaction to us breaking up."

"Oh…I know that, Ray. I didn't mean to say that at all," he quickly replied.

She was almost sure she had his meaning right, but had said her piece and didn't want to argue.

"Can I help you? It would make me feel worlds better if I could do something nice for you. Just…because."

Rachel sighed. "I'd appreciate your help, Eric. I really would."

"Great. Here's what we need to do. Fax me a copy of that letter, and I'll need some other documents. Charlie's birth certificate…" He reeled off a long list and Rachel made some quick notes. She was good about saving important papers and thought she could find most of it…somewhere.

"I'll call his attorney and let them know I'm representing you now," he added. "I'll let him know we're going fight this, Rachel. And he's not going to win."

Those were just the words Rachel wanted to hear. But somehow, hearing Eric say it made her feel…confused.

"She's hired a lawyer. Someone here, in New York. Pretty good firm," Mark Warner reported. "According to him, she doesn't want to talk at all. She just wants you to disappear."

Don't I wish I could, Jack answered silently.

"Jack, are you there?"

"I'm here. So…what next?"

"We can sue. We'll figure out some spin on your bad behavior. We'll investigate her, thoroughly. Down to the last freckle. Turn up any possible flaw on her character. Even a parking ticket..."

"I told you. She's a great mother. Mature, responsible..." *Pretty damn all-around wonderful.* "You won't get anywhere with that."

"Let me worry about that, Jack. Everyone has something in the closet that looks bad in court. All we need is one unpaid bill, an overnight with a boyfriend. Just the fact that she shacked up with you so quickly could look bad to a jury. If we play it right..."

The very suggestion made Jack instantly crazy.

"No investigators! No...snooping into her past or present. No using our relationship to smear her. Or you can send me your final bill right now, Mike. I mean it!"

"Okay, calm down. I thought you wanted your son, Jack? I thought you wanted to be part of the boy's life? It's not going to be easy—or pretty—persuading this woman to let you into the child's life. Maybe you need some time to think about how you want us to handle this. How you want us to win. Just don't tie my hands too much, okay?"

"I get your point. I'll get back to you."

Jack slammed down the phone and squeezed his eyes shut. He'd made a perfect mess of things and now he was paying the price. He felt just sick over it. And ever since he'd gotten back to New York...he hated his life.

He wished he had taken a picture of them, Rachel and Charlie. Why hadn't he thought of that? He closed his eyes, picturing them clearly in his mind—Rachel walking toward him across the lawn on a sunny afternoon, Charlie balanced on her hip. Her beautiful Madonna-like face, her long, flowing hair and tantalizing body. Charlie's nearly toothless smile and big brown eyes, just like his own.

He wished he could turn back time and be there, knowing what he knew now. He would give up everything he had in his real life to be that other Jack Sawyer. The guy in the broken-down truck, scrambling to earn a dollar. Who didn't own a thing, but was the luckiest man in the world.

Letters flew between the two law firms for the rest of the week. Copies would come to Rachel over her fax machine and she nearly jumped out of her skin every time she heard it start up.

Eric promised her that they were making progress. But she couldn't see it. The letters all seemed the same angry accusations back and forth. Threats of legal action. Bigger and bigger packages of material compensation.

Even Eric had to pause and ask her to consider if she really wanted to turn down these offers.

Rachel insisted she wouldn't be bought off, all the while wondering if Jack would get Charlie away from her somehow, anyway.

Worst of all, she missed him. She ached for him. She longed for his touch, the sound of his voice. The feel of his body curled next to her in bed.

Not the real Jack Sawyer of course. But the man she had fallen in love with. The man who had made some passionate love to her night after night. Had that all been an act, too? It broke her heart all over again to think so. If so, she didn't even have those memories.

Did he miss her at all? Or was it just Charlie? It seemed that Charlie alone was the focus of his quest. She felt so used...and discarded. She just wouldn't be tricked and manipulated by him again.

"I have some good news for you," Julia told Rachel over the phone Thursday morning.

"Please, anything. I need some good news this week."

"I think I found the perfect tenant for you. She came in yesterday, answering an ad we had in the paper for a book-keeper. She's a single mother. A widow, actually. Isn't that so sad?" Julia explained, "She needs a place to live and I know you've been looking for more help at the store. My job is only twenty hours a week, so maybe she can work for you, too."

Rachel had been looking to hire someone else besides Lucy, who couldn't really commit to a regular schedule. She needed someone willing to help with sales a bit and help manage her accounts. Especially since the holidays were coming. Her business was getting so busy and her Web site would soon start a flow of internet sales.

"When can I meet her?" she asked.

"I can bring her over today. What time is good for you?"

They set up a time for Rachel to meet Carey Moorland and also agreed to have dinner together.

Rachel hung up, feeling the day was getting off to a promising start. She hoped it would be a trend.

When Julia and Carey arrived around five o'clock, Charlie was still having his nap, so Rachel had some time to talk to her about her sales and bookkeeping experience.

She gave Rachel a résumé and two letters of recommendation. But more than that, Rachel liked her instantly.

"This is such a beautiful store," Carey said, looking around. "I haven't had much sales experience. But I'd love to work here. Whatever you'd like me to do, I can do it."

Carey was all Julia had promised. And even sweeter than Rachel had expected. She brought along her baby, a little girl a few months younger than Charlie. Rachel saw a perfect playmate.

Rachel waited in the shop, while Julia showed Carey the cottage. They soon emerged and both were smiling. Rachel felt a huge relief. It looked like she finally had a tenant. That was one less problem to worry about.

That night Rachel had dinner at Julia's house. The legal battle had been going on a week and Rachel felt totally worn out.

"Rachel, eat something. You look terrible," Julia coaxed her.

"Gee…thanks."

"Oh, you know what I mean. I'm worried about you," Julia admitted. "The way you're going, you'll make yourself sick over this. Then where will you be?"

Rachel sighed. She knew her friend was right. "At least I've lost few pounds. I fit into all my old clothes again."

"It's not a diet I'd recommend," Julia replied.

Julia had made Rachel's favorite dinner, good old-fashioned pot roast and mashed potatoes. Rachel couldn't eat a bite. She had barely eaten or slept for days and, unfortunately, looked it.

"I'm not sure what to do any more. I feel as if I might be depriving Charlie of so many advantages, but I still don't want Jack to win. Not after what he's done."

"It's a very hard choice to make, Rachel. I don't know what to tell you."

"Jack's lawyers want to have a meeting. I'm not sure if that would even help."

"What does Eric think?"

"He thinks he should go without me. But I'm not sure about that, either. I don't think he can really speak for me. I don't think he really understands how I feel about…everything."

"Which is?" Julia's knowing gaze pinned her.

Rachel sighed. "I'm getting confused."

"At least you're willing to admit it."

Rachel did feel confused. If only Jack could give her some small sign that he cared for her, that what had gone on between them hadn't been an act, she would have more sympathy for his side of the situation. She never had any doubt that he loved Charlie, and would be a loving father.

"I'm not sure anymore if I have a right to deprive Charlie of a father. What if he ends up hating me when he's older?"

"You have to think about that, Rachel. I don't think Jack will ever give up. He loves Charlie. As much as you do," she added.

Rachel knew that was true. If she was in Jack's position, she would fight a hundred years if necessary to be reunited with her son.

A few days later, Rachel called Eric. She'd made her decision.

"I want you to set up a meeting. I want to be there, too. I can't drag this out any longer. Jack isn't going away and...I can't stand the suspense," she admitted.

"All right, Rachel. If that's what you really want."

She heard the hesitant note in Eric's voice, but was glad that he didn't try to talk her out of it.

"Yes, that's what I want. The sooner the better."

"I'll call them this morning. We don't want it to happen too quickly," he added. "We'll need to prepare. It's important that we don't have any surprises in this type of face-to-face situation, Rachel."

He didn't want her to have a meltdown when she saw Jack and agree to anything.

"I understand," she said simply.

"It would be best if you come down to New York a day early. So we could review what we want to say."

She was sure that Eric would have some carefully written script he wanted her to follow. She didn't know why they couldn't go over that on the phone. They'd done well so far with phone calls and e-mails.

"It would be hard to leave here in the middle of the week. I don't think I can find anyone to watch Charlie for that long, either."

"You can bring Charlie. I'll find a good sitter for him. You can both stay at my apartment," he offered.

Now she understood. As much as she'd made it clear that they had no romantic future, and had insisted on paying for his legal counsel, he obviously still believed he had a chance to win her back.

"Eric, I'm sorry. I'm thankful your help and support...but

I don't want to mislead you. What I told you a few weeks ago, when you visited me is still true. My feelings aren't going to change. If you don't want to represent me anymore, I understand."

Eric silence told her all she needed to know. She had guessed his feelings accurately. She was sorry to hurt him, but not sorry she'd told him the truth.

"Of course I want to represent you, Rachel. I'm not going to drop the case now. I pressured you. I didn't mean to. Maybe after everything is settled, you'll see things differently."

Rachel didn't answer. She didn't think so. She hoped by then he would feel differently about pursuing her.

If only I could fall in love with him again, she thought. Life would be so easy. But her heart still belonged to Jack. And probably always would. Her sad and sorry fate.

That night, Rachel found an e-mail from Eric. The meeting was set. Just two days away. One o'clock on Friday. She stared at the message and took a long deep breath.

Had she done the right thing, forcing a show down with Jack? Or was she being too impatient?

It was hard to know for sure.

E-mails and phone calls flew back and forth between her and Eric for the next twenty four hours. He did send a script and gave her instructions to memorize it.

Rachel asked Julia to drill her Thursday night. Julia insisted on making dinner again and Rachel went over with Charlie. She was a bundle of nerves and glad for her friend's support.

"I don't know if I can go through with this. Maybe I should cancel. Eric told me that I could. He said it would be a good strategy."

"Rachel, I think the time for moves and countermoves is over. I think you have to just sit down with Jack and figure this out. It's Charlie's future, you know?"

Rachel nodded. "Yes, I know. I'm not going to back out. I have to do it. For his sake." She sighed and tossed the legal script aside. "I hate to face Jack looking like such a wreck, though. I still don't know what to wear...."

"Don't worry, by the time we get through with you, he'll be knocked off his feet. Again," she added, with a wink. "Come upstairs. Let's go through the closet and then we'll work on your hair and makeup."

Julia closet was full of possibilities. The two women agreed that the best choice was a tailored black suit that made Rachel look quite intimidating. Julia worked on her hair and makeup next, making Rachel's blue eyes smoky and mysterious-looking and her fine lips drawn with a rich berry color.

"Wow...I look..."

"Fantastic. He'll be speechless. And so will all his lawyers," Julia promised. "Remember, just let your lawyer do most of the talking, and just be yourself, Rachel. It doesn't get better than that," Julia promised.

Rachel hugged her. "Thanks...thanks for everything."

Julia shrugged. "What are friends for? Don't worry, it will all work out fine."

Rachel sighed. She didn't see how it could, but she hoped so.

It had gotten late and Rachel needed to go. She had to leave early for New York and drop Charlie off at Lucy's house where he would stay for the day.

Charlie was sleeping when she lifted him from the car seat and brought him into the house. He already had his pajamas on and she gently laid him down in his crib and waited a moment until he nestled down.

As she crept from his room, she heard a knock on the back door. She thought it might be Carey. She'd just moved into the cottage and Rachel wondered if she needed anything.

She ran downstairs and pulled the door open.

It was Jack. He stared at her, unsmiling.

"Hello, Rachel...can I come in?"

Rachel took a step back, feeling as if her heart had nearly stopped beating. "What are you doing here? I'm not supposed to talk to you, Jack...you know why..."

She started to close the door, but he reached out and held it open.

"Rachel, please." His voice was low and persuasive. "I just want to talk to you, face-to-face. Without all the lawyers in between." He paused and frowned. "You're alone, aren't you?"

"Of course I'm alone," she replied.

"I saw a car in the driveway. I thought Eric might be around again."

That was Carey's car, she realized, but she didn't stop to explain it to him.

"No, I'm alone. Except for Charlie..."

The word hung in the air between them. She could see Jack's expression change at the sound of his son's name, his face transformed by a flash of yearning.

She sighed and stepped back from the doorway. "All right. You can come up. For five minutes. I can't see how this situation could get any worse," she admitted.

She walked into the living room and Jack followed. She stood as far from him as possible, folding her arms across her chest. She wasn't wearing Julia's power suit any longer, but still felt as if she might be. She was glad she'd let Julia fool with her hair and makeup tonight, too. At least it hadn't gone to waste. At least she looked better than she felt inside and Jack had no idea of how she'd suffered over him.

"So? What is it? Some new offer? Charlie will live in Disney Land for six months out of the year?"

She almost thought Jack was going to smile. His gorgeous mouth twitched at the corner. She felt a wave of longing sweep through her body. The rest of him looked just as appealing as ever, unfortunately.

"No, but if that would persuade you, it can be arranged."

"Come on, Jack. I'm waiting. What do you want to say to me face-to-face that's so important?"

"Rachel, I came all this way to say one thing. Something I should have had the courage to tell you a long time ago. I love you, Rachel. I love you with all my heart and I love Charlie too. More than I ever thought possible…."

She stared at him. His words left her speechless. Breathless. Her head spinning in disbelief.

Then suddenly she came to her senses. He still thought she was so gullible and naive, didn't he? Well, he wasn't going to trick her again. Not that easily.

"Why should I believe you for one second, Jack?" she argued back, though she wanted to believe him with all her heart and soul. "That is the last maneuver of a desperate man."

"I am desperate," he cut in. "Desperate to be with you again. I don't want to just share custody of Charlie, shuttling him back and forth between us. I want to share a life with you and our son."

He stepped forward and gently gripped her shoulders.

Rachel stood looked up at him, melting under his touch, unable to answer. She felt as if she might be dreaming.

"I was a jerk, Rachel. A coward. A plain fool. I should be horsewhipped for the way I tricked you. But I've never been in love before," he explained. "Not really. It flat out terrified me. How much I felt for the both of you. I didn't know what to do. I knew if I told you the truth, you'd throw me out on my ear. And I couldn't stand the thought of that, not seeing you and Charlie anymore."

Rachel sighed. She didn't know whether to laugh or to cry. "Julia told me you would say that."

"Julia's a smart lady. I always liked her. I love you, Rachel. I want you to marry me. I promise I'll do everything I can to make you happy. I promise I'll be a good father to Charlie."

"I know you will," Rachel answered quietly. "I never doubted that, Jack."

She threw herself into Jack's arms and squeezed him tight. "I love you Jack. I probably fell in love with you the first minute you walked into the shop," she admitted, whispering the long held secrets of her heart. "I don't care if you are a world-famous architect and not the irresponsible drifter and carpenter you claimed to be. I still love you and want to be your wife."

Jack laughed, holding her close, the sound filling her with warmth and familiar passion. Who said a woman can't have it all? With Jack in her arms and their child sleeping peacefully in the next room, Rachel knew she was the luckiest woman in the world.

Jack kissed her passionately, his hands and lips hungry for her touch. Rachel answered his caresses, feeling she couldn't get close enough. They were soon in her bedroom, their clothes trailed across the floor. She lay down and wrapped her legs around his hips, unable to wait a moment longer for their searing joining.

Stars collided behind her eyes as they moved together in a sweet ancient rhythm. She heard Jack's murmurs of love somewhere in the distance as she trembled in his arms. They were one, melting and merging, two souls intertwined in a blue-white flame of ecstasy.

Afterward, they laid together in the darkness, unable to sleep. Jack was too excited, talking about the future. Things they'd do together, trips they'd take with Charlie.

Rachel assumed he'd want her to give up her business and move back to the city.

"Of course, we'll always come back to Blue Lake," he said.

"You mean...to visit?"

"Don't you want to stay here? What about your shop? I'd never ask you to just abandon all that, Rachel."

She leaned up one elbow and stared down at him. "What about your firm, Jack? Don't you need to be in New York?"

He sighed and folded his arms behind his head.

"I thought I did. But they survived pretty well without me

while I was here with you. I love Blue Lake. It's the perfect place to raise Charlie. A much better environment than the city. I've always been a workaholic, Rachel," he confessed. "Now that I have you and Charlie, my priorities are completely different. I want to find a big old farmhouse somewhere out side of town. Then I'll base my work at home and go down to the city or visit projects whenever necessary. What do you think of that plan?"

"It sounds perfect." She hovered over him, preparing to give him a kiss. "Let's make sure there are plenty of bedrooms for Charlie's brothers and sisters."

"Absolutely." He pulled her across his chest, the hard lines of his body molding and merging with every inch of her. "Just one rule. From now on, we make babies the old-fashioned way."

She smiled, then kissed him hard, feeling him ready to share their passion all over again.

"Agreed. The old-fashioned way is *definitely* more fun."

* * * * *

Enjoy a sneak preview of
MATCHMAKING WITH A MISSION
by B.J. Daniels,
part of the **WHITEHORSE, MONTANA** *miniseries.*
Available from Harlequin Intrigue
in April 2008.

Nate Dempsey has returned to Whitehorse to uncover the truth about his past...

Nate sensed someone watching the house and looked out in surprise to see a woman astride a paint horse just on the other side of the fence. He quickly stepped back from the filthy second-floor window, although he doubted she could have seen him. Only a little of the June sun pierced the dirty glass to glow on the dust-coated floor at his feet as he waited a few heartbeats before he looked out again.

The place was so isolated he hadn't expected to see another soul. Like the front yard, the dirt road was waist-high with weeds. When he'd broken the lock on the back door, he'd had to kick aside a pile of rotten leaves that had blown in from last fall.

As he sneaked a look, he saw that she was still there, staring at the house in a way that unnerved him. He shielded his eyes from the glare of the sun off the dirty window and studied her, taking in her head of long blond hair that feathered out in the breeze from under her Western straw hat.

She wore a tan canvas jacket, jeans and boots. But it was the way she sat astride the brown-and-white horse that nudged the memory.

He felt a chill as he realized he'd seen her before. In that very spot. She'd been just a kid then. A kid on a pretty paint horse. Not this one—the markings were different. Anyway, it couldn't have been the same horse, considering the last time he had seen her was more than twenty years ago. That horse would be dead by now.

His mind argued it probably wasn't even the same girl. But he knew better. It was the way she sat the horse, so at home in a saddle and secure in her world on the other side of that fence.

To the boy he'd been, she and her horse had represented freedom, a freedom he'd known he would never have—even after he escaped this house.

Nate saw her shift in the saddle, and for a moment he feared she planned to dismount and come toward the house. With Ellis Harper in his grave, there would be little to keep her away.

To his relief, she reined her horse around and rode back the way she'd come.

As he watched her ride away, he thought about the way she'd stared at the house—today and years ago. While the smartest thing she could do was to stay clear of this house, he had a feeling she'd be back.

Finding out her name should prove easy, since he figured she must live close by. As for her interest in Harper House… He would just have to make sure it didn't become a problem.

* * * * *

Be sure to look for
MATCHMAKING WITH A MISSION
and other suspenseful Harlequin Intrigue stories,
available in April
wherever books are sold.

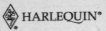

Silhouette®

SPECIAL EDITION™

Introducing a brand-new miniseries

Men of
Mercy Medical

Gabe Thorne moved to Las Vegas to open a
new branch of his booming construction
business—and escape from a recent tragedy.
But when his teenage sister showed up pregnant
on his doorstep, he really had his hands full.
Luckily, in turning to Dr. Rebecca Hamilton for
the medical care his sister needed, he found
a cure for himself....

Starting with

THE MILLIONAIRE
AND THE M.D.

by *TERESA SOUTHWICK,*

available in April wherever books are sold.

HARLEQUIN® *Romance*®

presents

The Wedding Planners

Planning perfect weddings…
finding happy endings!

Amidst the rustle of satins and silks, the scent of red roses and white lilies and the excited chatter of brides-to-be, six friends from Boston are The Wedding Belles—they make other people's wedding dreams come true….

But are they always the wedding planner…never the bride?

Who will be the next to say "I do"?

In April: Shirley Jump, *Sweetheart Lost and Found*
In May: Myrna Mackenzie, *The Heir's Convenient Wife*
In June: Melissa McClone, *S.O.S. Marry Me*
In July: Linda Goodnight, *Winning the Single Mom's Heart*
In August: Susan Meier, *Millionaire Dad, Nanny Needed!*
In September: Melissa James, *The Bridegroom's Secret*

*And don't miss the exciting wedding-planner tips and
author reminiscences that accompany each book!*

www.eHarlequin.com   HRI7507

HARLEQUIN®
Super Romance®

Celebrate the joys of motherhood!
In this collection of touching stories,
three women embrace their maternal
instincts in ways they hadn't expected.
And even more surprising is how true
love finds them.

Mothers of the Year

With stories by
Lori Handeland
Rebecca Winters
Anna DeStefano

Look for Mothers of the Year,
available in April
wherever books are sold.

HSR71482

REQUEST YOUR FREE BOOKS!
2 FREE NOVELS PLUS 2 FREE GIFTS!

SPECIAL EDITION®
Life, Love and Family!

YES! Please send me 2 FREE Silhouette Speâal Edition® novels and my 2 FREE gifts (gifts are worth about $10). After receiving them, if I don't wish to receive any more books, I can return the shipping statement marked "cancel." If I don't cancel, I will receive 6 brand-new novels every month and be billed just $4.24 per book in the U.S. or $4.99 per book in Canada, plus 25¢ shipping and handling per book and applicable taxes, if any*. That's a savings of at least 15% off the cover price! I understand that accepting the 2 free books and gifts places me under no obligation to buy anything. I can always return a shipment and cancel at any time. Even if I never buy another book from Silhouette, the two free books and gifts are mine to keep forever.

235 SDN EEYU 335 SDN EEY6

Name	(PLEASE PRINT)

Address	Apt. #

City	State/Prov.	Zip/Postal Code

Signature (if under 18, a parent or guardian must sign)

Mail to the Silhouette Reader Service:
IN U.S.A.: P.O. Box 1867, Buffalo, NY 14240-1867
IN CANADA: P.O. Box 609, Fort Erie, Ontario L2A 5X3

Not valid to current subscribers of Silhouette Speâal Edition books.

Want to try two free books from another line?
Call 1-800-873-8635 or visit www.morefreebooks.com.

* Terms and prices subject to change without notice. N.Y. residents add applicable sales tax. Canadian residents will be charged applicable provinâal taxes and GST. This offer is limited to one order per household. All orders subject to approval. Credit or debit balances in a customer's account(s) may be offset by any other outstanding balance owed by or to the customer. Please allow 4 to 6 weeks for delivery. Offer available while quantities last.

Your Privacy: Silhouette is committed to protecting your privacy. Our Privacy Policy is available online at www.eHarlequin.com or upon request from the Reader Service. From time to time we make our lists of customers available to reputable third parties who may have a product or service of interest to you. If you would prefer we not share your name and address, please check here. ☐

SSE08

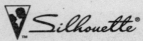